# THE FEROCIOUS FORCE

# THE FEROCIOUS FORCE

UNSTOPPABLE LIV BEAUFONT™ BOOK 8

SARAH NOFFKE

MICHAEL ANDERLE

LMBPN Publishing
PMB 196, 2540 South Maryland Pkwy
Las Vegas, NV 89109

First US Edition, July 2019
Version 1.02, March 2020
Print ISBN: 978-1-64202-364-0

THE FEROCIOUS FORCE TEAM

**Thanks to the JIT Readers**

Daniel Weigert
Nicole Emens
Jeff Eaton
John Ashmore
Dorothy Lloyd
Crystal Wren
Kelly O'Donnell
Peter Manis
Misty Roa
Micky Cocker
Jeff Goode
Larry Omans
Angel LaVey

*If I've missed anyone, please let me know!*

**Editor**
The Skyhunter Editing Team

*For Trudy.*
*The first day we met, you called me a tiger.*
*Still my favorite college class ever. And the one that flamed my*
*fire for writing.*
*— Sarah*

*To Family, Friends and*
*Those Who Love*
*to Read.*
*May We All Enjoy Grace*
*to Live the Life We Are*
*Called.*
*— Michael*

## CHAPTER ONE

The rough waters of the Atlantic Ocean licked at the boat, making it rock violently. Still the giant stood firmly, not even swayed off balance by the turbulent seas. Bermuda Laurens knew the waters were trying to push her away. She could feel their uncooperative nature. That was actually what had lured her to this very spot.

Lifting the binoculars to her face, she peered through. Bermuda shook her head, not having seen the signs she'd been looking for for over three days. Soon she'd have to pull up the anchor and give up.

The giant had been all over the world. Seen things most couldn't even imagine. And yet, being in this spot off the Canary Islands filled her with constant dread. The chilly winds ran up her back, messing up her curly hair.

Pulling her brimmed hat from a nearby cubby on the bridge, she stuck it on her head. Bermuda could withstand the unforgiving winds and salty air another several weeks, but what she couldn't face was the empty feeling that plagued these waters. Still, she was determined to give this voyage a fair chance. She'd give up because she'd found nothing, but not because she was afraid of that which lurked somewhere under these seas.

"Where are you?" Bermuda muttered to herself, still searching the surface of the waters.

"You know talking to yourself is a sign of insanity?" Plato asked, suddenly having materialized on the bridge of the ship next to the giant.

Unsurprised by the feline's sudden appearance, Bermuda unhurriedly brought the binoculars down, still peering at the waves in the distance. "Insanity is a relative term. Do tell me, how is craziness measured?"

"Usually it's when one has a disconnect from reality," the lynx offered, sniffing the ocean air.

"Right, and since we both live in a world where we have realities of our choosing, who is to say we are connected to the right reality? Therefore, depending on the observer, we could be sane or insane."

Neither the giant or the lynx said anything for a long minute while they listened to the sails flap in the wind.

"May I make a suggestion?" Plato asked.

"That is the reason I asked you here," Bermuda said sternly.

"I know what you want me to suggest, but this is regarding the ship," Plato explained.

"What about the ship?"

"It isn't cloaked," Plato answered.

Bermuda rolled her eyes. "Of course, it isn't. How were you going to find me if it were?"

"Excellent point," Plato stated. "However, now Decar Sinclair can find you as well."

Bermuda spun around, searching the horizon for another ship.

"You won't see him," Plato offered. "He was wise enough to disguise his vessel."

Bermuda narrowed her eyes, throwing her finger into the air. A moment later the ship was cloaked in fog, making it impossible for it to be seen by others. "I don't appreciate your implying that I wasn't wise in hiding my ship."

"Was that how you took my words, Bermuda?"

"You can call me Mrs. Laurens, or better yet, call me nothing at all, lynx."

"And yet you were the one who summoned me," Plato stated.

"Are you going to tell me where the lost city of Atlantis is?" Bermuda asked, her tone full of irritation.

"Why would I know where that is located?" Plato asked innocently.

"Don't you play games with me, lynx," Bermuda said vehemently. "You wrote about it."

"I believe you're confusing me with the philosopher. It happens all the time."

"You may be able to fool others, Aristocles, but not me."

"Oh, well, then I don't have to tell you that cloaking your ship in fog will make it hard to find with the naked eye, but not for anyone using radar," Plato said casually just as a blunt force rocked the side of the ship, nearly tossing Bermuda over the side. The lynx stayed firmly in place, as if glued.

Catching herself on the rails, the giant looked over her

shoulder, her eyes smoldering. "The evil magician dares to strike a blow at my ship?"

"It appears so," Plato answered as another blast hit the stern of the ship, sending the bow straight into the air before it slammed down again. Water splashed over the sides, flooding the deck. Bermuda was tossed around as if she were a paper doll and not a giant who was over seven feet tall.

"I've really had quite enough of that man for one lifetime," Bermuda said, pressing her fingertips to her temples and closing her eyes.

"Might I suggest…" Plato began, cutting into her focused thoughts.

Through the chaos of water spraying and waves crashing into the rocking boat, Bermuda cracked one eye open. "What? What do you suggest?"

"Well, it's just that if you are looking for Atlantis, and it is under the surface of this water, you might not want to create a fault line that produces a tsunami, even if it *is* intended to capsize the enemy's ship."

Bermuda deflated, knowing she should have thought of that. Plato was incredibly helpful when he wanted to be, she remembered. Then she recalled that he hardly ever wanted to be, which had been the inherent problem when they were a team.

"Do you have any better ideas?" she screamed through the howling wind.

"Not presently."

She seethed. There was the Plato she knew. Of course, he knew how to handle Decar Sinclair's ship, but where would be the fun in telling her that?

Bermuda pointed into the distance, drawing her power from the earth under her feet, several leagues under the sea. To her surprise, a blast of magic pooled in her being. If Atlantis wasn't below, then it was another mecca full of incredible energy. She used the large reserve of her magic to create a twin illusion of her ship far in the distance. It raced the opposite way toward the Canary Islands as if trying to seek aid after being assaulted multiple times.

Scanning the area where the blast had come from, Bermuda didn't see her enemy's ship materialize, but she did spy the tell-tale signs in the currents of the water as a large vessel changed course, charging after the phantom ship she'd created.

"Well, that won't last for long, but at least it will buy me some time," Bermuda said, letting out a weighty breath of relief.

She cleared the fog from the front of the ship, again looking for signs of the lost city. It had to be close, she reasoned, but nothing she did seemed to give her any new clues. It burned her up that a magician had found the lost city, or that was her assumption anyway. And they'd used the city no one could find to hide what was probably the most important book in the world—the *Forgotten Archives*.

"Where are you?" she muttered again to herself.

"You're doing it again," Plato observed.

"Talking to one's self is also a sign of intelligence," Bermuda offered.

"Intelligence is relative, dear Bermuda. How can it be measured when no one knows what an intelligent mind must consists of?"

"The ability to reason and use logic," Bermuda answered at once, conviction in her tone.

"Oh, but now you muddy the waters by speaking of ability when we were talking about intelligence."

"Muddy the water? Really? You've been hanging around Liv Beaufont too long if you're making repugnant puns," Bermuda said with a scowl. "And I'd argue that intellect involves the ability to deduce and assess and many other things."

"And yet, my experience states that intelligence is more like a storehouse in a person's mind, whereas reasoning and deduction are skills."

Bermuda sighed. "I haven't missed your games with semantics in the least."

"You wouldn't call a reservoir and a dam the same thing, would you?"

"Well, of course not," Bermuda said with great offense.

"Then it's not semantics," Plato said at once. "Intelligence is the reservoir, and reason and deduction are the dam. You can't fill the lake or keep it balanced without both."

Bermuda sighed. "Although I'll admit your experiences on this planet far exceeds mine, right now I think you're wrong."

"It doesn't matter if I am or not, only that I helped loosen the gears in your brain long enough that you take your focus off finding Atlantis."

"For what reason?" Bermuda asked.

"So you can, in fact, find it."

"That makes no sense," she protested.

"I agree, and yet that's how most things in life work,"

Plato offered. "When we search for things, we push them away. When we have lost something, it stays hidden from us. But when we invite in confusion, as I did with my lecture on intellect, we usually find that clarity tags along, slipping through the door before we shut it."

"You know, all those centuries, and you still make no sense," Bermuda said dryly.

"Oh, well, it's too bad that I couldn't be more helpful."

"I find it hard to believe that you're at all remorseful, lynx."

"Note that I didn't apologize. I only stated that it was unfortunate that I can't illuminate more for you," Plato said simply. "Maybe you'll have better luck on your own—as long as your intellect doesn't steer you wrong."

The lynx disappeared at once, leaving Bermuda standing alone at the bow of the ship. She was about to curse the feline for offering her zero help, as usual. However, suddenly Plato's words ran through her mind, with emphasis on certain words: I can't *illuminate* more for you. *You'll* have better *luck on your own*. As long as your *intellect* doesn't *steer* you wrong.

Bermuda didn't know if she was going insane, as Plato probably intended with his riddles, or if she was onto something. She reasoned that she didn't have anything to lose either way.

Closing her eyes, Bermuda pulled up the anchor with a flick of her finger. Then she rotated the ship's wheel three-quarters of a turn to the right, two full rotations to the left, and just a smidge to the right. The directions weren't anything she'd read about or reasoned, but rather just random guesses. She opened her eyes and strode like a robot straight to the bow of the ship. As luck, or rather the farthest thing from logic, would have it, in front of the ship was a small patch of water that was strangely illuminated.

Bermuda shook her head, cursing the lynx and silently praising him. Whether he intended to help, she'd never know. He worked mysteriously like that.

Holding her hand over the side of the ship, she muttered an incantation. The water around the boat began to tremble. The sky turned gray. Lightning struck in the sky, followed by thunder. And then, from under the water, a small object exploded, landing on the deck of the ship.

Bermuda let out a long sigh. She could hardly believe it. She'd found the book—the *Forgotten Archives*. The one that captured the real history of mortals and magicians. The one that held the reality of what happened with the Great War.

This was what they needed to free mortals from the curse. Once this book was activated, everyone would know what had happened. But first, they needed to be able to see magic again.

## CHAPTER TWO

The corridor at the front of the House of Seven appeared longer today. Liv Beaufont was absolutely certain it was lengthier than usual. It was a common trick the House pulled for no apparent reason.

On some days, the rooms were larger or smaller, or furniture was missing or rearranged. When Liv was a child, it had been exciting, never knowing what a room would look like when she entered it. Presently, though, it always made her pause. The House never did anything without reason. When Sophia's dragon's egg had been inside the House of Seven, the entry door had increased in size, which had been impressive since it was already the width and height of a small house.

If the House's entrance hall was longer, it meant something. What, Liv didn't know.

She ran her fingers over the ancient symbols adorning the gold walls, enjoying the way they sparked and danced, making a circular pattern.

"That's new," Liv said, noticing that the symbols were

acting differently than usual. They always lit up for her and vibrated, as if the language were activated by her touch. However, she'd never seen the symbols spiral like they were doing, creating a funhouse effect on the wall. "I wonder what this could mean?"

"You're talking to yourself," Plato observed, appearing beside her.

She shook her head. "No, I'm talking to you."

"I wasn't here a few seconds ago when you made your first remark," Plato explained.

"About the pattern with the symbols being new?" Liv asked.

He nodded.

"Well, then how do you know what I said?" Liv challenged.

"Touché."

"Seriously, do you know why the language of the Founders is spiraling like this when I touch it today?" Liv asked.

Plato tilted his head to the side as if seeing the pattern from a different angle would help. "Have you had a lot of salt today?"

Liv huffed, dropping her hand from the wall as she turned to face the lynx. "What does that have to do with this?"

"It doesn't. I just noticed that your fingers look a little swollen."

Liv rolled her eyes. "You're ridiculous. And no, I haven't had too much salt."

"Are you sure? What about those nachos you had while Netflixing last night?" Plato asked.

Liv put her back to the feline. "Seriously, if you say you're out for the night, why can't you actually be out?"

"I was," he stated smugly.

"Then how do you know what I ate for dinner?"

"Because you left the takeout boxes in the trash."

"Why are you going through the trash?" Liv asked.

"How else am I going to know what you had for dinner while I was away?"

"You can simply ask," Liv answered.

He shook his head. "There's no fun in that."

"You're very strange. And I thought you were always watching me, even when you are away. How come you didn't know what I had for dinner using your spyware or whatever you've got?"

"I was in a place where I couldn't get good reception on my Liv cam," Plato stated.

"Oh? Like where, I wonder?"

"Other things you could wonder about would be how much sodium was in those nachos last night," Plato said.

"I'm sure it wasn't—"

"Three times your daily allotment," Plato said, cutting her off. "And that's for your intake as a magician."

"Are you lecturing me about my eating habits?" Liv asked.

"Even though you're allowed to eat five thousand calories a day, they don't have to be from junk."

"Rory says desserts are best for magic restoration," Liv argued.

"And you had a pile of fried chips covered in melted cheese with steak. There was no sugar in it."

"Your point?"

"Chocolate mousse would have filled your magic more and not made your fingers swell."

"Are you really advising me to eat sweets over nachos?" Liv asked.

"I wouldn't dream of telling you what to do," Plato said. "But yes, I'm trying to help you to make better choices. If you want to live for more than one century, then you do have to be mindful about what you put in your body."

"It's funny that you're worried about queso being my demise," Liv said with a laugh. "You were there when Shitkphace was trying to kill me, right? Or when Subner explained that I must cross molten lava on my next mission? Or when that druggie tried to cut me on the street this morning as he passed? My day job is pretty dangerous in case you haven't noticed."

"Fixing appliances does come with some risks," Plato said matter-of-factly.

"I meant my other day job," Liv said dryly. "So, what do you make of the new behavior of the ancient language?"

"What do *you* think it means?"

Liv gave him a scolding look. "That I need a new sidekick."

"Can you read it?" Plato asked, ignoring her remark.

Liv squinted at the symbols. "I used to be able to, but for some reason, I'm struggling with it today. Anyway, it always says pretty much the same thing about the ancient chamber."

"Are you sure?" Plato asked, an undertone to his voice.

Liv pulled out the Warrior ring and sighed. "No, apparently I'm not." She ran the large gem over the symbols that were spreading out in large spirals, half-expecting them to translate into the message she'd read here a hundred times. However, this time, the words were different.

"*Stop the One and you'll free us all,*" the founders' words read.

"The One?" Liv asked. "Who could that be? And free us all? Is that referring to mortals?"

"I couldn't say," Plato answered.

Liv gave him a sideways glare. "You mean, you won't say."

"Actually, isn't it strange to you that the founders' message here has changed?" Plato asked.

Liv thought about that for a moment. The House of Seven constantly changed, like the long corridor here. Why shouldn't the messages written in the ancient language change? But if they did, that begged one specific question. "Yeah. Like, who is writing it? I'd normally say the Founders, but are they doing that from beyond the grave? And how?"

"All good questions," Plato agreed.

Liv shrugged. "Well, I'll have to think about them. I don't want to be late for the meeting with the Council."

"But you're always late," Plato questioned.

"Yes, when Adler Sinclair is presiding over things." Liv ambled toward the other side of the corridor, in the direction of the Chamber of the Tree.

"Oh, and he's absent, so you have no reason to be late and therefore irritate him," Plato guessed.

Liv spun. "Unless you think my tardiness will cause stress to Bianca Mantovani?"

"I think your breathing does that," Plato said simply.

Liv swelled with pride. "I do try to get under that witch's skin."

She continued on, stopping when almost to the Door of Reflection. "Is it just me, or is the Black Void a bit… Oh, I don't know, *spirally* today?"

The blackness ahead still had a foreboding quality to it, but today it was moving like a storm cloud on a dark night.

"Something does seem to be brewing," Plato answered.

Liv took a step toward it, but like a cord was attached to her navel, she got a swift jerk backward. Glaring behind her, she expected to see that someone had yanked her back. There was nothing.

"I guess I'm not supposed to enter the Black Void today," she stated. "It just seems to mirror the pattern the ancient language is making."

"Then it sounds like more investigation is needed," Plato offered. "I'd advise not to enter a place that you know nothing about, and no one else can see."

"By that logic, many discoveries wouldn't have been made," Liv said with defiance. "Like North America, for instance."

"And think how much better things might have been then," Plato offered.

Liv shook her head. "Okay, fine. I'll stay away from the spiraling blackness that makes my insides crawl with unease. If you insist."

"I absolutely do," Plato said calmly.

Taking a step toward the Door of Reflection, Liv prepared herself for what would come next—her deepest, darkest subconscious fears revealing themselves in her mind's eye.

## CHAPTER THREE

Liv stepped through the door that was like a pool of water to find herself wearing a tight evening gown. In the dream-like state, she turned around, looking at herself in a mirror. The dress was snug in places, making it hard to breathe, and worse than that, the neckline scooped dramatically, so her boobs were on display.

A painful pinching sensation spread across her toes. Liv held up the heavy material of the dress to find she was wearing strange torture devices.

*Those are high heels,* a voice in her head said.

Liv did a full turn, horrified by the color of the dress she was wearing—freaking hot pink. Her head was suddenly churning with horror. It sent painful waves of panic down her spine. Filled her stomach with dread.

And then she realized her nightmares were about wearing a dress.

This must be about Rudolf's wedding.

She shook off the violent emotions and stepped

through the Door of Reflection and into the Chamber of the Tree.

The strangest noise greeted Liv's ears. She's never heard it in the chamber with the council. It was laughter.

With a scrunched brow, Liv looked around, noticing that Stefan and Haro were chuckling and many of the others in the room wore amused expressions.

"So then I told the elf that if he thought he created nightmares, he must have been responsible for me," Stefan stated. "Then I shot him with my bow and arrow."

Haro slapped his hand on the bench in front of him. "That's priceless."

"What does the High Elf Council think about it? That you're taking out their most wanted to earn their favor?" Bianca asked, a pinched expression on her face as if the tight-fitting gown she was wearing smelled of pickles. Liv shuddered, thinking of the awful dress she had been wearing in the image in the Door of Reflection. She had to stop herself from clawing at her flesh like she had on the conforming dress again. With relief, Liv glanced down at the t-shirt and jeans she was wearing under her loose cape.

"I haven't met with the High Elf Council yet," Stefan answered.

"Why not?" Lorenzo asked.

"Because my strategy is to take out all the direct threats to the elves to earn their favor first," Stefan stated.

"But then you will make them invincible," Lorenzo said, sounding suddenly nervous.

Stefan turned his head to the side as if he hadn't heard the council member quite right. "Ummm...my idea is to earn their loyalty. I can't do that unless I take out their enemies. All of them."

"Or you could just take out a few and earn it that way," Lorenzo countered.

"I was thinking—"

"I agree with Councilor Rosario," Bianca said smugly. "I think we are wasting our resources by having you take out all the enemies of the elves. You should try to approach the negotiations now."

Hester leaned forward, giving Bianca and Lorenzo an expression that could mostly be described as saying, "Are you two as batty as hell?"

"I'm certain that Warrior Ludwig knows the right strategy here," Hester argued. "He's made it farther than anyone else so far with these negotiations. I say we let him continue at his own speed."

"Although it appears that he's made it farther," Lorenzo stated, "I think it's an illusion. He's simply yet to meet a roadblock, but one could be ahead."

"I'm okay with Warrior Ludwig continuing as he has," Clark stated with new confidence.

Haro, Raina, and Hester agreed at once, nodding.

Bianca's and Lorenzo's expression showed their disapproval. Before they could protest, Raina swung an invisible hammer, making an echoing sound around the chamber.

"Then it's been decided," she sang, "Warrior Ludwig will continue to fight evil while also forging a path to a true alliance."

The other council members laughed, cheering for Raina's enthusiasm. It was like a window had been opened in the chamber, making it feel like a spring day.

Liv gave Stefan a cautious look. "Did I miss happy hour before the meeting? Everyone is in a good mood."

"Not everyone," he said from the corner of the mouth.

She knew what he meant immediately. Bianca and Lorenzo seemed angrier than usual as they scrolled through their codices.

"Should I stay to see your show?" he asked.

With a minute shake of her head, Liv said, "There won't be anything to see."

"That's hard to believe," he said, rocking back on his heels, his hands behind his back.

"Ms. Beaufont," Bianca said, regarding Liv with her usual disdain. "Why are you here? We thought you had cases with Father Time."

"I do," Liv stated with finality.

"Then why are you here?" Lorenzo asked.

"Oh, to tell you that I will be working with Father Time for a bit," Liv said. Diabolos swooped down, pecking just inches from Liv's feet. She smiled meekly at the council, realizing that he was calling her out as a liar.

Hester waved off any frustration, continuing to laugh good-naturedly. "I'm sure whatever you're doing with Father Time is none of our business. We will leave you to do what you've got to do."

Really? Liv wondered cautiously. There wasn't any eye-rolling or insults being hurled her way. She wasn't sure what to do with herself.

"I think it's obvious that Ms. Beaufont isn't being forth-right with us about her projects," Bianca said.

"I'd like to be," Liv began. "However, Father Time

prefers that I keep my work private since he's not sure who can be trusted."

Bianca rolled her eyes.

*There it was*, Liv thought.

"We are the Council for the House of Seven," Bianca said in a scolding tone. "We can obviously be trusted with the details of your cases."

"I don't know," Haro argued, combing his hand over his chin. "If Father Time says you should keep them private, Warrior Beaufont, I would encourage you to do so. We all believe we can be trusted, but that's beside the point. Sometimes, there are details we are simply not ready to comprehend."

Liv blinked up at the council member, wondering if he knew about her case regarding the Mortal Seven. There were many in the magicals who weren't ready for *that* information. It would shatter their world. It would create chaos. That was why Liv knew when the time came, she had to reveal the information in the most constructive way possible. Mortals shouldn't be punished, and magicians had to find a way to assimilate the change.

Finally, Liv nodded, backing away from her spot. "Okay, well, I'll be back when Father Time releases me."

She nearly tripped over Jude, the white tiger, who had somehow soundlessly laid himself out right behind her. Liv righted herself before stepping on the animal. She spun around, her heart suddenly racing, and nearly fell onto Diabolos.

Liv's chin flipped up to find Stefan and the council regarding her with curious stares. Bianca's mouth was actually hanging open.

"I've never seen anything quite like it," Haro stated, indicating to Liv's predicament of being sandwiched in between the regulators in the Chamber of the Tree.

"Me either," Clark said, shaking his head at her.

"What could it mean?" Raina asked.

"That she's simultaneously telling the truth and hiding something," Lorenzo offered.

"She's lying," Bianca fired, throwing an accusatory finger at Liv.

"I-I-I'm not," she said as Diabolos pecked at her boot. She felt something press into her calf and noticed that Jude rubbed his face against her.

"Did you wash your clothes with raw meat again?" Stefan asked with a chuckle.

Liv shook her head. She was too perplexed to make light of this situation.

"Is there anything you want to share with us, Ms. Beaufont?" Lorenzo asked, then added, "Regarding your work for Father Time or anything else."

Carefully Liv stepped away from the tiger and the crow, backing toward the Door of Reflection. "Not at this time. But as soon as I can, I will," she said and sped for the exit.

## CHAPTER FOUR

Adler Sinclair wasn't as young as he used to be. The climb to the summit of the Matterhorn had proven that. However, he had been able to rely on his magic to make the trek, unlike Guinevere and Theodore Beaufont, who'd had their magic locked when they were here. That was the last time Adler had been on the Matterhorn. The last time he saw the Beaufonts. The last time anyone had seen them.

Adler knew it was preposterous, but he felt like their ghosts were there, haunting him. Each time a wind howled past his ears, sounding strangely like words—threats—he told himself it wasn't real. That the hike was making him crazy. That the guilt was eating him up.

He kicked snow out of his path, thinking he couldn't go on any farther. The harsh conditions, even during the warm season, made the trek arduous. This wouldn't have been so excruciatingly painful if Indikos hadn't deserted him. For miles, Adler had told himself how wronged he'd been to have his dragon disappear. Indikos had grown increasingly distant over the last several months.

Adler sighed. *Who was he kidding?* The dragon had always been distant, even though all of Adler's research had said miniature dragons and their companions had a bond akin to one with a rider. Indikos had always been there, but never truly present. *And now he wasn't even that,* Adler thought bitterly.

This time of year, mortal hikers were bountiful on the Matterhorn. It annoyed Adler that he had to cloak himself in order to stay hidden from them. That had burned through magical energy he might need for other things. It just proved that mortals were useless, causing more problems than they were worth.

Thankfully, most of the mortals were on a different path that would take them to the Solvay Hut, a refuge for hikers. It was the mortal version of the broadcasting facility—a tiny house with inadequate amenities.

Adler was headed for the facility Talon had constructed ages ago in the opposite direction. It wasn't a shabby hut that offered respite to weary travelers. It was a sturdy structure that housed one of the most important pieces of magical tech in the history of mankind. And not only was it hidden from mortals, but it was also cloaked to prevent magical creatures from finding it.

The signal that broadcasted inside the facility wasn't electronic, like most thought of magic tech these days. There were no wires or circuits. It was mechanics and gears, coupled with a rare magical force. Together they combined to create a signal that when broadcast out into the world, prevented mortals from seeing magic.

It was a simple enough theory: Interrupt the signals in their brains that were receptive to magic, and then they couldn't see it. That had been the first thing the God Magician had done after winning the Great War. Then he'd erased the history and buried it forever in the *Forgotten Archives*. The book and the magic tech had been his creations. There was a reason he'd won the war and overthrown the entire House—he was better than the rest.

*And so was I,* Adler thought.

Soon he and Talon would take over the Council, and rule as they were meant to. That was the way it had been supposed to be, but Father Time had stopped Talon, putting him into hiding all this time. That had given the Royals time to recover, and the ancestors of the Founders slowly came into power.

By the time Talon's relatives were old enough to take their positions as Councilor and Warrior, the House of Seven was well formed. That had made it tougher for the Sinclairs to rise to power, but not impossible. Adler had made great progress in his time, protecting that which the God Magician had started. It was their greatest family secret, and the one worth protecting for all time.

Things hadn't gone entirely to plan. What was supposed to be the House of Sinclair had become the House of Seven. The Royals had returned to power. However, the signal was still broadcasting, and the *Forgotten Archives* were still hidden in the lost city of Atlantis. And Father Time was back, which meant he could be killed. Then the One would rise to full power, as he had always intended.

A cold, forceful wind roared by Adler's head.

*Die,* the wind seemed to whisper.

He swung around, believing someone or something was there.

Sharp gray rocks stretched in all directions, covered in patches of snow. There was no one in sight. *Not even a repugnant mortal.* Adler shook his head, believing that the loneliness was starting to get to him. He hadn't wanted to be the one who went to the Matterhorn, but he knew he was the only choice. Protecting the signal was important.

For generations, the Beaufonts had tried to stop this. Before Guinevere and Theodore, there had been the brothers, and before them was another team. The Sinclairs and the Beaufonts had been fighting for too long, according to Talon. The Beaufonts were one of the founding families, and for some reason, they never seemed to accept the "truth." Even the Takahashis, another founding family, had gone along with things when they came to power. Sometimes they seemed confused when they heard "the House of Seven," like it didn't sound quite right, but they always let it go.

Not the Beaufonts, though. Generation after generation stuck their nose where it wasn't supposed to go. They never seemed to accept that this was the way things were. They always asked too many questions. But that was all about to stop.

Olivia Beaufont had gone too far.

Adler had felt little remorse about killing Guinevere and Theodore. Their children, Ian and Reese, though? That had been harder. However, if Olivia came after him, he would care very little about what he had to do to stop her from prying anymore. This stopped with her.

Like an explosion in his belly, Adler felt the conviction that accompanied his thoughts spurring him on when he was close to quitting. The Sinclairs had let this go on for too long. It was time to end things. To make them go the way it had always been meant to be.

Talon had thought of so much. He'd invented the magic tech responsible for the signal. He'd created the book that contained the *Forgotten Archives*. However, he hadn't thought to end the problem that had caused everything from the beginning—mortals.

Adler had reasoned that Talon had gone soft on mortals since it was he and the other six magical families who had constructed the House, along with seven mortals. However, things had been different then. There had been a reason to form an alliance between mortals and magicians.

The giants had been out of control. The gnomes had refused to cooperate. The elves had been an unyielding force. That was why the House of Fourteen had been formed—to control the other races. And then the reality unfolded—mortals thought they owned some of the power. They tried to control things and voted on magical matters when they far exceeded their experience. They had over-stepped their boundaries, and that was when the Great War had begun.

But it would all end with Adler.

He nearly stumbled with excitement when he rounded the bend to see the facility Talon had created all those years ago. Inside the two-story structure was the signal responsible for inhibiting mortals from seeing magic and therefore involving themselves in matters they knew nothing about. It had worked well enough all this time. However, when Adler was done with it, it would fix all their problems.

For some reason Talon had never wanted to disclose to Adler, he'd refused to end mortals. *That was the simple solution,* Adler had always thought. But Talon had fought him whenever he pushed the matter, saying that killing all mortals wouldn't work.

Well, Adler was ready to prove him wrong. Get rid of mortals, and then magic could exist without any barriers. All he had to do was tweak the signal. Then it wouldn't matter if Olivia Beaufont made it to the summit of the Matterhorn or uncovered the *Forgotten Archives* since all of the mortals would be dead already.

## CHAPTER FIVE

"Wait," Sophia said in disbelief. "Let me get this straight. If something happens to mortals, or the longer that magic stays hidden from them, the higher the chance that it will disappear forever?"

Liv nodded. "Yes. It's the element they control. We all feed our energy into our element somehow."

"Fueling it?" Sophia guessed.

"That's right, according to Papa Creola," Liv answered. "And the longer humans are disconnected from magic, the more it will decrease. Apparently, it's on a sharp decline all of a sudden."

"So there is an even better reason to stop whatever is preventing mortals from seeing magic," Sophia said, affectionately stroking her dragon's egg.

"Well, if the fact that erasing the real history and brainwashing mortals wasn't enough," Liv said, stooping to peer under her bed.

"He's under there still," Sophia said.

Liv peeked under the messy bed, making a mental note

that she needed to clean up the dust bunnies, to find the miniature dragon staring back at her, his orange eyes glowing. "Hey, Indikos, I recognize that my place is no palace, but you can come out at some point. I brought you some fresh meat since you can't hunt."

Sophia, the egg, and Adler's dragon had been staying with her. It would have been a bit cramped before she did the remodeling. Now her once-tiny studio was like a penthouse apartment, with adequate areas for guests to relax. However, Indikos preferred the cramped, dusty place under the bed.

"He doesn't want to talk," Sophia said plainly.

Liv grunted as she pushed up from the floor. "Like he said in your head, 'Hey, I don't want to talk,' or that he simply didn't say anything and you inferred the rest?"

"It's hard to describe how the telepathy with dragons works," Sophia explained. "With my dragon, I get specific messages that I know are his thoughts. With Indikos, it's more of general ideas and feelings."

"Hmmm," Liv said, thinking. "Well, I've got neither of those, and I need to travel across the world with the creature, so I think I'm going to have to find a solution. Communication might be important when I'm being attacked by ten-headed monsters and caught up in cyclones."

"How do you know you'll have to face such things?" Sophia asked.

Liv opened Bermuda's book, *Mysterious Creatures*, and pulled it toward her. "I don't, but that's usually how my missions go. Murphy's Law keeps me on my toes."

Liv was unsurprised when she opened the seemingly

endless volume straight to the page on miniature dragons, or as Bermuda called them, majunga. Several times Liv had flipped through these pages but hadn't found anything that told her anything new. She was about to give up when she noticed two of the pages were stuck together. Careful to not rip them, she encouraged them apart.

Sophia crawled over from her place on the floor, instantly curious what new information Liv had found.

"According to Bermuda…" Liv said slowly, scanning the new pages, "there is an herb that a non-dragon rider can take which could potentially make it so they can talk to dragons."

"It's crazy that you just found that and we were just talking about it," Sophia said, leaning over Liv's shoulder.

"No, that's pretty much par for the course," Liv stated. "I've gotten over the ironic aspects of the timing in my life."

Sophia gave her egg a curt nod, like the dragon inside of it had just said something. "She would never."

"Ummm…" Liv said, her gaze shifting between the little girl and the big, blue egg. "She would never what?"

"He had just said something about how you're getting desensitized to this world, and he hopes you don't become jaded."

Liv scrutinized the egg. "Just because I joke doesn't mean I've started to take all this for granted. It's just that my life and all its absurdities make me laugh."

Sophia giggled. "It makes us laugh too."

"Well, I'm glad I can be an entertainment for you two," Liv stated. "By the way, are you going to keep calling your dragon him and he or do you have some idea for a name in the meantime? I realize you're waiting to name him fully until you've met officially, but maybe just a placeholder like Billy or Jimmy or Dwight?"

Sophia grimaced. "None of those sound like dragon names."

"That's the point," Liv said with an eye roll. "That way they don't accidentally stick."

"Well, I get the reason for having a name to refer to him—"

"Especially because even without being hatched, he's a part of the conversation," Liv cut in.

Sophia nodded. "And yes, he's definitely part of things. But I don't want to get in the habit of calling him one thing and then change it."

"I understand that," Liv stated. "He is your dragon. However, I might call him Eggar or Eggy or Eggward, if that's okay."

Sophia giggled. "It's fine with me, but he doesn't like it so much."

"Tell him to come out of that shell and stop me, then," Liv challenged.

Sophia's gaze grew distant, and then she shook her head. "He says nice try, but he's not ready yet."

Liv sighed. "Fine. Can't rush perfection, I guess."

A knock at the door made Sophia's giggling halt. Liv glanced up.

"Hey, you girls busy?" John called from the front.

"No, we're back here in the bedroom," Liv called.

A moment later, John materialized in the doorway, a snorkeling mask on his head. "Gosh, it took me nearly a full minute to walk across your place, Liv. Been doing some more expansion, I see."

"Well, I felt bad that Sophia was cooped up in here, so I added the fountain to the foyer," Liv said.

"And an atrium with an outdoor corridor for that fountain," John added, glancing over his shoulder. "Is that a slide off the dining room?"

Sophia continued to chuckle.

"Well, like I said, I wanted to ensure Sophia got exercise," Liv stated meekly. "And what better way to arrive for dinner than by slide?"

John lowered his chin and gave Sophia a serious expression. "She's feeding you real food, right? Not just stuff out of boxes or nachos?"

"We had nachos last night!" Sophia cheered.

"With a side salad," Liv corrected. "And I know how to cook now."

"I know you're trying," John said, looking around. "I'm not interrupting you two, am I?"

"Oh, no," Liv said, waving him off. "I was just teasing Sophia's unhatched dragon and trying to coax the small dragon I kidnapped out from underneath the bed."

"Just a regular Tuesday," Sophia added.

John shook his head. "Well, my request might seem a little mundane to you two, but I wanted to show off my new vacation clothes and see if you approve. Will you take a look and give me your opinion?"

Liv waved him into the room. "Show us."

She'd convinced John to use the profits from the sale of the pinball machine to take a luxurious tropical vacation. It had been too long. He deserved it more than anyone.

He stepped out from the other side of the doorway to

reveal himself in an orange and red Hawaiian shirt with trunks to match, and a blue snorkel and fins.

"How are those clothes any different from your normal stuff?" Liv asked, hiding her laughter.

"Oh, you," John said, putting his fists on his hips. "I'm a tourist on the beaches of Waikiki. Don't I look like one?"

"Slap some sunscreen on your nose, and the locals will be lining up to scam you," Liv quipped.

"That's the beauty of a vacation, right?" John asked. "Going to a place you're not from so others can take advantage of you, selling you things at higher prices than they're worth?"

Liv nodded. "I'm glad you settled on a beach vacation rather than some lonesome cabin in the woods."

John sighed. "Yeah, I guess tropical will be more fun. I'm all set for the most part."

Liv popped to her feet. "I have forgotten to ask Rory about watching the shop. I would do it, but I have this whole—"

"Saving the world business," John said, cutting her off with a smile.

"I was going to say taking Indikos to his new home, but yes, along the way, I have to reconnect mortals to magic," Liv stated.

"Well, my dates for the vacation are flexible, so whenever Rory is free will work for me," John imparted.

Liv grabbed her things before placing a light kiss on Sophia's head. "I'm sure he can do it. He never goes anywhere."

"But this is his busy season at work," John protested.

"Which is?" Liv asked.

He wagged his finger at her. "Rory made me promise not to tell you what he does professionally. He says it's a game you two are playing."

"He's playing this game," Liv grumbled. "I'm being ridiculed on the side for not knowing enough about my friend."

"You two are so cute," John remarked.

Liv patted him on the shoulder as she left. "I'll be back in a bit. I'm going to stop by and make arrangements with Rory. Will you make sure the dragon rider eats?"

"As long as she promises that her dragon will never eat me," John said, followed by another delightful giggle from Sophia.

Liv pulled on her cape as she left the apartment. She'd worried about having Sophia and the egg stay with her, but it had been wonderful so far. She felt warm and complete when she curled up in her place at night to the sound of her little sister's soft snores. And folding her mortal life with John together with her magical one with her family made her feel so expansive, the way she pictured it would be in the future, once mortals were released from the brainwashing.

## CHAPTER SIX

A book flew through Rory's open front door as Liv approached. She ducked, and the volume soared over her head and into the yard. At the threshold, she had to dart out of the way to avoid getting hit by a tray, a basket of yarn, and a stuffed bear.

"What's going on?" Liv asked from the porch, partially hiding behind the side of the house.

Rory had his back to her, his shoulders rising and falling dramatically as he took labored breaths. When he turned around, his face was red, and his eyes were crazed with worry.

"Rory, are you okay?" Liv asked, about to rush forward but stopping herself. Rory liked his space, especially when he was upset.

"It's my mum," Rory said, his eyes scanning the mess at his feet.

"Bermuda?" Liv asked. "Is she all right?"

Rory shook his head and then corrected the movement, nodding. "I think she's fine for now. She sent me a message that said she was being pursued by Decar Sinclair, but that she had found and taken the book."

For a moment, Liv thought her head was going to explode with information. "Decar? He's pursuing her?"

After everything that had happened with Adler stealing Sophia's egg, this seemed like all Liv needed to assume the Sinclairs were behind this whole conspiracy. As if reading her thoughts, Rory shook his head, a stern look on his face.

"We don't know why Decar is after Mum, and we can't jump to assumptions," Rory stated.

"Oh, do you think it's because he's lonesome on the road and just wants to have a cup of coffee?" Liv asked, her tone dripping with sarcasm.

"I know Adler and Decar are no good," Rory stated. "But we don't know if they are out for their own selfish gains or if they are behind everything or if they are working for someone else. It's important to remain objective."

Liv motioned to the mess on the floor. "Is that what you're doing? Being objective?"

He raked his hand through his frizzy hair. "I'm trying, but Mum sounded nervous in her note."

"What did she say?" Liv asked.

From his jean pockets, Rory pulled out a crumpled piece of paper and handed it to her.

Liv took it hesitantly. "What, did she send it via carrier pigeon?"

"Something like that," Rory answered.

Unfurling the note, Liv pulled it up close to her face to read the compact handwriting.

*I have the book. Decar is pursuing me, but he is at least a step behind. Don't worry, and don't come after me.*

*Love,*

*Mum*

"Book?" Liv asked. "What's this about a book?"

Rory shrugged. "She'll have to explain it to us when she returns. I'm not sure. I'm going to go find her and help her get back."

Liv held up the note. "I believe she said not to go."

"But she's in danger," Rory nearly whined.

"How can you tell? She says Decar is a step behind her."

From the same pocket, he pulled out another crumpled note. "In her last message, she said that Decar was pursuing her but he was at least a few steps behind. Now he is only a step."

Liv tilted her head to the side. "Don't you think you're mincing words just a tad?"

Rory shook his head, then grabbed for a bag on the floor and started to fill it with items. "I have a bad feeling about this. And if the book is the key to uncovering the real history, then Mum will be in even more danger. Decar and whoever he's working with won't let her get away with it. They'll pull out every stop. I just know it."

Often Liv argued with Rory. Sometimes it was for her own amusement, because she enjoyed seeing that frustrated look flit to his face. Then there were other times when she absolutely disagreed with him. However, in this situation, she knew not to argue. Rory might have been fearful because it was his mother, but he was basing it on instinct. She knew how valuable gut feeling was and would never tell her friend to ignore it.

"I'll go too," Liv said, picking up some clothes off the floor and stacking them on the coffee table. "Where is she? Do you know?"

"I'm not certain, but I have a tracker I'll use when I set off to find her." Rory dropped his bag on the ground, glancing around in confusion. "And no, you can't go. You have your own job to do. If you don't bring down that signal on the Matterhorn, there's little reason for us to uncover the real history."

Liv knew he was right. It was tough for her to allow him to go off to help Bermuda, although she didn't like it when others tried to interfere in her plans. "Okay, well, what can I do to help?"

"Stay in contact with me," Rory said. Taking a pad and pen from a nearby shelf, he handed it to her.

Lifting an eyebrow, Liv held up the pad he'd given her. "What do you want me to do with this?"

"Write me messages on it. It's an anywhere pad."

"And send them to you via carrier pigeon or Pony Express?" Liv asked.

He pulled a pad from his back pocket. "No, I'll get the message here on my own pad. Just the same way I got Mum's messages."

"Couldn't we just use cell phones?"

Rory shook his head. "No, this is much safer. It's more secure."

"Before you head out," Liv began, pulling her copy of *Mysterious Creatures* out of her pocket, "I needed to see if you have a certain herb. I've never heard of it." She opened the book to her place marker and squinted. "It's called sturi…something."

"Sturistriderfen," Rory supplied.

Liv gave him a look of disbelief. "How did you get that from my broken mispronunciation?"

"I know how you think," Rory stated. "And you have a dragon you need to communicate with, so I figured it out."

"How do you know I have a dragon I need to talk to?" Liv asked, curiously, realizing that she hadn't had a chance to tell Rory about Sophia's egg or Indikos or really hardly any of the newest developments.

"Well, it's a majunga, to be specific," Rory corrected himself.

Liv narrowed her eyes at the giant. "How do you know that? I haven't told you anything about it or getting Sophia's egg back yet."

He sniffed the air. "How could I not? You reek of majunga. And that's good news on the egg. I knew it would come back to Soph. The two are magnetized to each other, so there was little way that he couldn't."

"But then does that mean that Adler will come after Indikos, his majunga?" Liv asked.

Rory shook his head, giving her a cautious expression. "I can't believe you took his dragon."

"His dragon sort of begged for my help," Liv corrected. "And it was the way to get Sophia's dragon back, which by the way she's named 'Todd.'"

Rory's expression told him he didn't believe her about the last part. "And no, I don't believe Adler will be able to come after his dragon. If the majunga was asking to be taken, then it was not magnetized to Adler. Otherwise, the act of formally separating them would cause both great harm."

"Wow," Liv said, shaking her head. "I never realized how the bond between a dragon and their rider or person worked."

"It's a magical force, Liv," Rory explained. "They are one. What happens to one affects the other, and vice versa."

Liv nodded slowly, trying to wrap her head around this strange new future unfolding before her little sister.

Rory pointed to the patio. "The herb you're looking for is in a planter between the rosemary and the lavender."

"Obviously," Liv retorted. "Because that's where I'd keep my dragon telepathy herbs."

"Where else should they go?" Rory asked, continuing to pack his bag.

Liv backed toward the door, wanting to stay and help and knowing she had her own mission that needed her attention. "Okay, but please write and let me know you're okay."

"I will," Rory said, continuing to stuff items into his bag.

"And let me know if you need my help."

"I won't," he replied.

"And tell your mum thank you."

Rory glanced up, a tender expression in his eyes. "We're all in this together now, Liv, so there's no gratitude necessary."

## CHAPTER SEVEN

Liv portaled as close to the island of Lehua as she could get. Unfortunately, that wasn't close enough. Hawaiki Topasna had ensured that visitors would have to cross many types of dangerous terrain to get to her.

Liv stared down at the molten lava bubbling a few yards away and shook her head. "So we cross the lava, then the jungle, and if we're not picked up by a cyclone, then we will arrive at Hawaiki's in time for dinner, I'm guessing," she said to Indikos, who was perched on her shoulder.

The dragon didn't answer. Instead, he flapped his wings and took off, soaring high into the sky.

Liv shook her fist at the small dragon. "Fine, I'll meet you on the other side. I prefer hoofing it anyway."

Apparently, the island of Lehua was known to be uninhabitable. It was supposed to be barren due to an extinct volcano. That was what the mortals believed, anyway. Well, and almost everyone else. There were few who ventured out this far on a hunch, just to see if the geography books were telling the right story.

They weren't.

Not only was the volcano not extinct, evidenced by the molten lava bubbling up by Liv's feet, but the island also wasn't barren, based on the tropical jungle that spread out on the other side. And then there were the calls of the many birds in the distance, which made Liv believe it also wasn't uninhabited.

She watched as Indikos' figure got smaller and smaller until he disappeared on the other side of the lava flow. Liv had tried to take a ship around this area to the side of the island where she believed the old elf to be, but that hadn't worked. Instead, she found herself going in circles until she gave up, deciding that wards were preventing her from getting to the island that way.

"So how do I cross molten lava?" Liv mumbled to herself, her brow already profusely sweating.

"Have you considered flying?" Plato asked, appearing beside Liv.

She shook her head at him. "I'm not a dragon. But hey… remember when you changed into a griffin? Maybe you can do that again and take me across this pond of hotness."

"I don't know what you're talking about." Plato held his nose up high like the smell of the burning rock was distasteful to him.

"Oh, that's right. We're playing that game again."

"Again?" Plato questioned as if she were the crazy one.

They fell silent, the only sound the gurgling of the lava. After a few minutes, Plato said, "You know, it might not be that hot, actually."

An abrupt laugh fell out of Liv's mouth. "Are you serious? I saw a fly evaporate when it was a few feet from the surface."

Plato shrugged. "Yeah, I guess it's pretty warm from this distance."

"You guess?" Liv asked, wiping her forehead of sweat yet again.

"Oh, well, I don't sweat or get warm, or really have any changes to my core temperature."

"Because?" Liv asked.

"Magic," he answered simply.

"And here I thought you were on one of those trendy supplements that all the housewives who are bordering on menopause on the West Coast are chugging."

As if he didn't hear her, Plato asked, "As I said, have you thought about flying?"

She tapped her chin. "You know what, I hadn't. Let me just manifest some wings, and then I'll be off. I'll meet you on the other side of the rainbow. Don't open the pot of gold without me."

Plato was not impressed with this retort, based on the way he batted his eyes. "You don't open a pot of gold. And I'm serious."

"Flying?" Liv questioned. "You think that's something I can do?"

"Well, maybe," Plato said, indecision strong in his tone. "There's only one way to find out."

"And if I fail, I'll land in a bunch of hot lava, which if you didn't know, will melt my bones," Liv stated.

"I don't sweat, but I know what lava does."

"Just checking."

"But seriously, have you tried a floating incantation?" Plato asked.

"I have, and I'm not really great at it," Liv answered. "I think I need to have mastered it to perform it over hot lava."

"From my ideology, there's no better testing ground than the one here," Plato said.

"Right, because the stakes are high."

"And you'll concentrate instead of day-dreaming about boys."

Liv huffed. "I've never. Not even once."

"There *was* that one time."

She faced forward, thinking about her options. "So, the floating incantation…do you think it could work?"

"It might."

"If it doesn't, will you catch me?" Liv asked, hope in her voice.

"I can't make any promises," he answered.

"Fine, so you want me to try my best, that's what you're saying?"

"I'm saying I have an appointment in about ten minutes, so it depends," Plato answered.

"Oh, you're insufferable."

Plato held up his paw like he was looking at his watch. "Would you look at that. My appointment just got shoved up by five minutes."

"That's fine," Liv said dismissively. "You can leave now. I don't need you."

She needed him to stay and rescue her if she failed, but she was not going to say that. Instead, she pressed her eyes shut and muttered the incantation over and over, hoping it worked. Hoping she knew how to control it. Hoping it ended differently than the last time she'd tried to float.

Ever since seeing Shitkphace float or fly or whatever he did in Venice, Liv had been trying to master the spell. It wasn't an easy one. When she'd asked Akio about it, his brow had furrowed, and he'd said she was much too young and inexperienced to try such a spell. Apparently, it wasn't something that people who weren't pilfering magical energy like Shitkphace tried, but Liv was determined to be just as badass as her opponents, without stealing the power to be that.

"I really hope this works," Liv muttered under her breath, wiggling her fingers by her side.

"You might want to open your eyes," Plato's voice cut in.

Liv shook her head, clenching her eyes shut even harder. "I'm trying to concentrate. Don't mess me up or I'll never get off the ground."

"About that…" Plato said, a hint of mischief in his eyes.

Liv's eyes sprang open. She was ready to admit defeat until she spied the empty air under her feet. Panic suddenly filling her being, and she kicked her legs like she was riding a bicycle. Automatically, she came down several feet, the bottoms of her boots melting from the close contact with the lava. Swimming through the air, Liv forced herself back up to where she had been when she opened her eyes.

"Might I suggest that you concentrate?" Plato said from the ground, although his voice sounded like it was in her head.

"Thanks for the tip," Liv said absentmindedly, trying to do just that. She focused on the patch of ground in the distance where she'd seen Indikos land. It was on the far side of the bright orange lava that flowed like water but didn't have the inviting appearance of a cool lagoon.

Never before had Liv been so aware of how her thoughts controlled all aspects of a spell. As soon as her focus drifted slightly, so did her placement above the lava, making heat crawl up her backside. Several times she had to block everything out and encourage herself to go higher. But then, like a child easily distracted by their environment, she'd gradually float back down until she was dangerously close to the lava.

Not until she was safely over ground bountiful with lush plants did Liv allow herself to descend, coming down to the surface like Mary Poppins did when landing. Liv didn't realize she was holding her breath until her feet touched the ground.

She'd done it! She'd floated. Or flew. Or whatever it was considered. That didn't matter, she realized as she looked back over her shoulder to where she'd come from. Plato was in the distance, his tail flicking back and forth, or so she imagined.

Indikos landed on her shoulder soundlessly, a disapproving look on his face.

Liv glanced at the dragon sideways. "Why, yes, I made it just fine. Thanks for inquiring."

The dragon might have seemed pretty heartless, but he had his moments. He pecked Liv's shoulder, and she realized something was in his mouth. Lifting her hand to his beak-like mouth, she waited for him to release it.

A cocoa bean fell into her palm. It wasn't a piece of rich,

milky chocolate, but it would have the same effect, restoring her magic.

Liv took it appreciatively, holding it up. "Thanks, pal. If I didn't know any better, I'd say you like me."

As if in answer, the dragon soared into a dense cluster of trees up ahead.

Liv shook her head. "Why do the magical creatures in my life have to be such helpful pains in the asses?"

## CHAPTER EIGHT

This jungle almost appeared like it was locked down, its vines creating a thick wall that prevented Liv from entering easily. She strode around the perimeter, looking for a way into the fortress. When an entrance didn't appear, Liv held up her hand and fired a spell at the thick wall of trees.

An opening formed, leading to a dark path into the forest. Liv took a step forward, but before she entered, the opening sealed up again.

"Cute," she said, not meaning it.

She didn't think floating would work again. For one, she'd need to lift over thirty feet in the air to clear the first line of trees. Also, she was worried about depleting her magical reserves without knowing what else she'd face on the island.

Considering her options, Liv tried to figure out the best strategy for entering the jungle. She couldn't help but think that the planning would be easier if she had input from a bird's eye view.

"Too bad I don't have a small dragon flying around somewhere," Liv yelled to the forest.

A moment later, a great shaking noise echoed through the branches. Liv expected Indikos to surface and maybe be ready to help. He didn't.

She had the herb that Rory had given her and thought it might be useful at helping them to strategize. However, the dragon had disappeared, leaving her to fend for herself.

"I just hope you show back up at some point," Liv said out loud. "I did come all this way for you, after all."

She realized that wasn't completely true as she pressed her hand to her mother's sword at her side. It gave her a sudden idea.

Pulling Bellator from its sheath, Liv faced off with the jungle. She reasoned that Hawaiki had put this spell on the jungle to keep magicians and other magical creatures away. Mortals wouldn't have been able to make it this far since boats wouldn't come to the island and portals were only allowed on the far end where she'd started from.

"Sorry, trees," Liv said, holding Bellator high before swinging it, cutting through the thick branches and vines.

To Liv's relief, the foliage didn't grow back. She continued to cut through the jungle, etching out a path, although she didn't know exactly where she was going.

"Again, it would be cool if I had a magical creature who was up high and could direct me," Liv muttered.

The tops of the trees shook violently. Liv was pretty sure Indikos was flying around in the canopy, lurking and messing with her. That was fine. He'd been through a lot, she reasoned. And he had been Adler's dragon, which meant he had some issues to work through. Still, the tiny dragon had asked for her help and done the right thing by helping them locate Sophia's egg. Liv had faith that Indikos would come around and be a good dragon. Currently, though, he was driving her bonkers.

Liv was slicing through the brush when she heard a loud buzzing beside her face. She swatted, her hand knocking against something. Twice more the bug harassing her zipped by her face.

After only a short distance, Liv was exhausted, covered in sweat, and growing dehydrated from the heat. However, her reserves weren't even close to being depleted. She assumed most magicians weren't used to such physical exertion, which made this a genius way for Hawaiki to keep people out, but it wasn't going to deter Liv.

Once she'd rested enough, she continued slicing through the brush, making progress to a better-lit area up ahead. A clearing maybe, Liv thought with hope. If Hawaiki's home was just up ahead, then this wouldn't be such a terrible mission after all. She'd be back home in time to have dinner with Sophia and Todd.

Feeling encouraged, Liv whacked through several thick vines just as a bug about the size of a penny landed on her arm. Startled at first by the large black beetle's sudden appearance, Liv swatted it away. Her hand knocked it to the ground, from which it glanced up at her and seemed to throw one of its legs into the air and shake it at her angrily.

Liv shook her head, wondering if she was hallucinating. Had she just offended a beetle? Maybe the fumes from the volcano were getting to her. Or she'd been bitten by a tree frog. Or the universe was again messing with her for its own entertainment. She sort of figured that God or the gods or whoever was ruling this planet had designed her life as a farce, making it suitable for reality television. She pictured that this entity watched over her with a tub of popcorn, laughing as the hilarity happened around Liv.

She was caught up in this daydream when another of the large beetles landed on her arm. Unconcerned with offending the creature, she brushed it off, sending it to the ground, where it scurried away. Liv could have sworn she heard muttering, and the beetle seemed to shake his head in offense.

"Sorry," Liv called after the retreating bug. "No free rides."

She continued to slice through the jungle, the clearing ahead growing more distinct.

"Crazy-ass place with its lava and thick jungle and easily offended beetles," Liv remarked to herself, realizing she had been talking to herself a lot more lately. She slashed down a large branch obstructing the path. "And, not that I should have to explain myself, those beetles have some serious pincers. I'd rather not become their dinner."

Ahead something shook the canopy overhead. Liv paused, wondering if Indikos was about to resurface.

The branches of a thick tree parted and a dark shadow fell on Liv. What appeared overhead wasn't Indikos. Not even close.

The creature that bore down on Liv was huge…

And ready to kill.

## CHAPTER NINE

Liv's breath hitched in her throat. Bellator shook in her hands. She cursed herself for thinking the beetles before were large. They had nothing on the giant one towering over her, its pincers clicking loudly.

The beast hissed, one of its antennas lowering, pointing straight at her.

"Heeeey," she said, doing her best to sound welcoming.

The beetle, which was easily the size of a truck, wasn't receptive to Liv's greeting. It shot forward, its pincers seeking to chop her in two.

Liv swung Bellator, jumping back several feet. She tripped on one of the vines she'd chopped, falling onto her backside. Bellator clattered to the side, out of her grasp.

Seizing its opportunity, the beetle shot forward, its pincers stabbing into the ground on either side of Liv's face, nearly impaling her. Pinned to the ground, Liv gazed up into the beetle's dark eyes.

"Hi," she said meekly. "Nice to meet you."

The beetle didn't seem as excited about the meeting. Or

maybe it had no manners, Liv thought as it hissed, sending a thick wet substance all over her face.

"Eeeww," Liv said, grimacing from the horrid smell of the snot-like liquid.

The beetle reared back on its hind legs, its pincers clapping together. Liv took her opportunity to roll out of the way. Her hands searched for Bellator, but it had slid under some thick roots.

Wiggling her hand into the small opening between the roots, Liv tried to grab the hilt, but it was wedged at a weird angle. She glanced up just as the beetle shot down like it had before. She abandoned her mission to the get sword and rolled into the hollowed-out trunk of a tree.

A second later, and she'd have been chopped in two. The beetle's pincers assaulted the bark, cutting into it, but the tree was thick enough to protect Liv.

She held up her hand, trying to think of a spell that would work on the beetle. After a quick deliberation, she sent a blast at it. That was when she realized that it didn't matter what spell she used. None of them were going to work. Magic was no good in the jungle. Not for chopping down vines and branches or for defending oneself against a giant beetle.

The trunk held firm after several assaults from the beetle as it slammed its pincers into the side. However, when it clamped them on either side and squeezed, the trunk cracked.

Liv was running out of options. She was without Bellator and magic and confined to the inside of a tree trunk.

The wood around her splintered, nearly breaking.

The tree she was using as a shield wasn't going to last for long. Liv knew she was going to have to make a run for it. However, the path through the jungle hadn't been fully forged yet, which meant she'd be slowed down navigating around vines and branches. Or she'd have to abandon her mission and run back the other way. And there was Bellator. She couldn't leave it behind.

Liv was busy trying to sift through her options when the beetle screamed, vibrating the ground under her feet. It reeled back, its pincers blindly chopping in the air. Liv was trying to figure out what had gotten into the mad beetle when she saw something swoop overhead. She could hardly make out anything from inside the trunk. Deciding to chance it, Liv ducked out of the trunk just as Indikos dove, attacking one of the beetle's antennas. The beast swatted at the small dragon, but he was nimble enough to avoid the collision. He disappeared into the jungle, making the beetle turn around to find its new enemy.

Liv didn't have a chance to dig Bellator out of where it was hidden. She pulled Inexorabilis from its sheath on the other side of her hip. A small shot of electricity pulsed through Liv's arm.

She knew what she had to do next. It was the only way to defeat the beetle, which thankfully was momentarily distracted as Indikos dove again, attacking its other antenna and severing it.

It screamed. Hissed. Reeled back on its hind legs. If it toppled over right then, Liv would be smashed.

Thankfully, the beetle dropped back down on its front legs, making the ground shudder from its enormous weight.

Liv didn't like what she'd have to do next, but it was the only way.

Indikos circled overhead, his eyes quickly shifting to Liv. He saw her, but did he know what she needed him to do?

She hoped that even without the herb, he shared her thoughts. Liv knew better than to take it now since Indikos was too far away for it to work.

The miniature dragon dove like a missile toward the ground, weaving between the beetle's legs. Unnerved by the strange attack, the beast reared again, its pincers high in the air.

Liv couldn't believe it had worked. She swung around to the front of the beetle, driving Inexorabilis into the monster's soft underbelly.

It screamed, its front legs flailing wildly.

Liv tried to move out of the way but was too slow. The insides of the giant beetle spilled onto her, slowing her down like she was suddenly in quicksand. Her progress at scurrying to safety was significantly stalled. Looking over her shoulder, Liv lunged forward, her chest constricting with panic. She was able to move a few feet through the mucus and guts, to safety…or mostly. When the beetle fell, it crashed on top of her, pinning her bottom half. The pincers landed inches from her legs. She glanced back, her mother's sword still in her hands.

The beetle was dead.

And its guts covered Liv.

She glanced up at Indikos, who was flying overhead. "Thanks, buddy," she said before letting her face rest in the soft earth as she caught her breath.

## CHAPTER TEN

It took Liv five whole minutes to peel herself out from underneath the beetle's dead carcass. Not only did its weight make it difficult to get out from under the body, but the slime still oozing from it made every move sloppy. The dirt under Liv had quickly turned to mud, moistened by the guts. Twice, she'd gotten to her hands and knees, only to slip and fall straight back onto her face.

When she finally made it to her feet, Plato appeared, looking her over casually.

"Don't say a word," she said, glancing down at her body, soaked to the core in slime.

"What?" he asked innocently. "I was only going to say—"

"If you mention anything about how I'm wearing bug guts, I'm going to stop buying cat food."

He shrugged. "Then I guess I'll have to eat nachos. Can you put anchovies on my half?"

"No," Liv said, kneeling to try to retrieve Bellator. She had to press her cheek into the dirt to see what was keeping the sword stuck. "We both know I don't share my nachos."

"Yes, it's been noted in your file."

Liv grunted, pushing and pulling to try to free the blade tangled in the thick roots. "What else does it say in my file?"

Plato licked his paw. "That you don't brush your hair."

"I do on weekends," Liv argued.

"You say inappropriate things when you're nervous," he continued.

"Or really just whenever," Liv added, feeling like she was going to have to dislocate her shoulder to free the sword.

"That you watch entirely too many Lucille Ball shows."

"That's inherently false. I watch the perfect number." With a swift jerk, Liv freed the sword, raising it victoriously into the air. "Ha-ha!"

"Good job," Plato said casually. "But just so you know—"

"Don't you dare say it," Liv warned, wiping her hand across her face but only making the damage worse. She was a sight to see, but unable to use magic, and with a pit of lava at her back and thick jungle before her, there was no way for her to freshen up.

"What?" Plato asked innocently.

"Whatever you do, don't comment on my appearance."

He blinked at her impassively. "Why would I do that?"

Liv sheathed Bellator and glanced down at her mud-caked hands. "Man, this bug slime stinks."

"Bug?" Plato asked.

Liv gestured at the giant beetle carcass, which had

started to steam, giving off an even worse smell. "Yes, I was referring to the bug I slaughtered."

"Oh, heavens," Plato said. "I totally didn't even notice it."

"Sure, you didn't." Liv picked up her mother's sword, trying to wipe it off as best she could before sheathing it.

"Beetles also aren't bugs," Plato offered. "It's a common misconception, but bugs have a different mouth structure than a beetle. Not only that, but—"

"This isn't really a good time for a science lesson."

"When would be good?" Plato asked. "I can pencil you in for later."

Liv looked at the blue sky, searching for the small dragon. "I don't know where Indikos went, but I'm hoping he shows back up soon."

"He's waiting at Hawaiki's hut," Plato stated.

Liv sighed with relief. "Thanks. Finally, something seems to be going right."

She started off toward the clearing she spied through the trees. It wasn't far.

"Oh, and Liv?" Plato said, stopping her.

She turned, thinking he might offer her more valuable information. "What?"

"You have something on your face," he answered.

She shook her head at the lynx. "You're dead to me, now."

"Cool. I'll see you at the house. But do wipe your feet before entering. Bug guts are hard to get off the floors," he said and disappeared.

## CHAPTER ELEVEN

Even sliding through tight clusters of leaves didn't remove the bug slime. Liv sort of felt like a car in a car wash with the giant brushes sliding by her as she squeezed through the jungle. However, when she came out the other side, she was hardly any cleaner than when she started.

Liv was grateful that she didn't have to go much farther to the clearing since she was having to walk a bit funny from the strange substances coating every crevice of her body. She studied the structure in the middle of the clearing, trying to understand exactly what it was. It wasn't quite a house.

It was a modest dwelling for sure, with its mud walls and grass roof. However, magic had definitely been employed in its construction, and also its appearance. When she glanced to the side, she could have sworn the building grew by several stories and looked like a polished home. When she peered directly at the house, it was merely a closet-like hut that looked ready to fall over at any second.

Several times, Liv slid her eyes to the side, and on each occasion, it appeared to be something different: a modern house with large windows and a box-like shape, an old Victorian with spires and gargoyles on top, a southwestern house with cacti and stucco, or a brownstone apartment in the middle of the city.

Around the outside of the house was mostly dirt, and there were loose tools strewn about. There was a lumpy large burlap sack sitting on a flat stone. The bag appeared like it had been left out in the rain too many times and had mold stains.

In back of the hut were a small field of crops and a few fruit trees. Indikos, unlike what Plato had said, wasn't sitting on the hut or anywhere in sight. Liv desperately hoped he showed up, or she was going to have to come up with another plan to get Hawaiki's cooperation. She would have taken the herb Rory had given her, sturistriderfen, but the book said the dragon needed to be present for it to work. Also, Liv's hands were completely covered in slime and guts, and she worried it would harm the herb's potency if she touched it. She'd just have to wait.

Liv realized she was about to knock on this elf's door looking like she'd been dipped in a vat of sludge. She pushed a bit of hair off her face and tried to brush off her shoulder like there was a tiny piece of lint on it instead of it being covered in thick slime. Her efforts were futile, making no difference to her appearance, but causing her hands to be even stickier than before.

She sighed in defeat as she approached the rickety door,

which looked like it had been taken from an old ship. Liv was just about to knock when something in her peripheral vision shifted. The lumpy burlap sack moved. Suddenly she realized that the old brown sack wasn't that at all, but rather an elderly woman.

"The owner of this place isn't home," the woman said, looking like a stone statue as she talked.

"Ummm..." Liv said, backing away. "I'm looking for Hawaiki Topasna. Is that you?"

The woman—Liv couldn't tell if she was old or a strange piece of furniture or beautiful—looked her over. Just like the house, the elf took on a different form depending on if Liv was looking at her straight on or from an angle.

"Where did you hear about Hawaiki?" the woman asked.

Liv was pretty certain this was the elf she was looking for, although she'd never met anyone so strange. She felt as though she couldn't see the woman clearly. Her figure kept morphing, and it was really messing with Liv's mind.

Searching around, Liv tried to locate Indikos. He wasn't in sight. She was going to have to play this just right, sensing the woman's uncooperative nature.

"I was sent here to find Hawaiki because I have something for her," Liv stated.

When the woman stood, she was not any taller than when sitting. Looking at her straight on, she appeared to be a dark, round woman with loose gray curls and a sturdy expression. However, even as Liv looked at her, she got flashed of other figures in her mind: a child, a young woman, a middle-aged woman, and then there was the elderly elf before her.

"There is nothing you can give to Hawaiki," the woman said, offense in her tone as she looked Liv over. "Why are you covered in that?"

Liv glanced down, a nervous giggle escaping her mouth. "Well, I took out that giant beetle that was terrorizing your island."

"You mean Rongo?"

Liv shrugged. "I didn't have a chance to catch its name since it was trying to slaughter me with its pincers."

"It was defending the island," the elf said, her eyes narrowing in anger.

"And I was trying to defend my life," Liv argued.

The woman trotted passed Liv, shaking her head with disappointment. "That's why I can't be around you magicians. Always killing everything."

"To be fair—"

Liv didn't get a chance to argue her point because the old woman disappeared into the hut and slammed the door.

Letting out a long breath, Liv stomped her foot. "Are you Hawaiki?"

The door opened an inch, and the old woman's brown eye stared at Liv. "Yes!"

She slammed the door again.

"But you said that Hawaiki wasn't home a moment ago," Liv stated.

Again the door peeled open. "I wasn't home. Now I am."

"Well, can I talk to you?" Liv asked. "I'm Liv, a Warrior for the House of Seven, and have an important request."

"No," Hawaiki said in a definitive tone, shutting the door again.

Liv sighed loudly. She should have expected this. "But I brought you a gift, and I've heard it's something you really want."

The elf stuck her head out of a window on the side of the hut that hadn't been there a moment before. "Where is it? If it's covered in Rongo's insides, I don't want it."

"It's not," Liv stated, glancing at the treetops around the clearing. "I've sort of momentarily lost it, but if you come out here and talk to me, I'm sure it will return soon."

"No deal." Hawaiki closed the shutters.

"Indikos!" Liv called to the trees. "Would you get your butt down here? I need your help."

Silence followed.

"Indikos!" Liv yelled even louder.

The shutters busted back open. "Would you keep it down? I'm trying to nap."

Liv didn't see how the woman could nap in the hut. It didn't look big enough to have a bed, even with the addition of the window. "I'm sorry. It's just that I came all this way to get your help. It's really important."

"So important that you had to kill Rongo?" Hawaiki asked.

"I apologize," Liv stated. "Was he your friend? He was trying to kill me, and I was only defending myself."

"No," Hawaiki said with great offense. "He was a pain in my ass, always tearing up my garden and destroying the natural vegetation on the island."

"So you're welcome—"

"But he kept people like you away, and therefore we had a truce of sorts," Hawaiki interrupted.

"Shouldn't I get bonus points for getting past your guards?" Liv asked. "I also got over the lava."

"Although impressive, you've wasted your time. Go away." The old elf closed the shutters once more.

Liv rolled her eyes dramatically. Of course, Hawaiki had to be an ornery, uncooperative old woman, and the gift she'd brought to buy her compliance had flown off.

"Why is it that the person I need help from is always against the idea?" Liv grumbled to herself, trying to think through her options.

Hawaiki's head popped back through the open window. "Whoever told you where to find me should have also mentioned that I wouldn't cooperate with whatever it is you want."

"They did," Liv stated dully. "Which is why I brought you a gift that's flown off."

"Too bad for you, then." Hawaiki's eyes sparked with curiosity. "Did you say that my gift flew off?"

Liv nodded, her eyes feeling like they were going crossed from staring at the woman, whose form constantly changed, and the house, which also kept shifting. "Yes. I brought you a miniature dragon because that was what Subner said you've always wanted."

The elf burst out of the door and was standing in front of Liv faster than she thought possible. "A majunga? That's what you brought me?"

"Yes," Liv said, defeat in her voice. "But he flew off into the trees, and I can't find him."

The elf looked Liv up and down disapprovingly. "Did you try to kill him like you did Rongo?"

Liv grunted. "No, I rescued Indikos, and he asked me to take him to someplace he'd be safe." She glanced around. "Although, I'm not sure that's this place. You'd have to prove you're fit to take care of him. He's been through a lot."

Hawaiki crossed her arms in front of her chest. "Of course, I'd provide a majunga with the perfect home. It's my dream to have one."

Liv nodded. "I know. That was why I brought you him, but he must be shy or something."

The elf shook her head. "No, he's not at all. He's watching me to see if he likes me."

It was difficult for Liv to suppress her expression, which accurately said, "Yeah, whatever, you crazy old woman."

To cover up her judgmental expression, Liv asked, "How do you know he's watching you?"

Hawaiki held a plump finger in the air, pointing. "He's right there in the trees."

Liv squinted in that direction, not seeing anything but branches and leaves. "If you say so."

Rounding on her, Hawaiki put her hands on her hips. "So you've come all this way to ask for my help?"

"Yes, and I brought you the majunga, although I get that it doesn't count if he stays away."

"It counts," the old elf sang, a hint of mischief in her voice. "Now it's my job to earn his favor."

"Oh," Liv said with relief. "Thank you. I need your help with—"

"When you look at my house, what do you see?" Hawaiki asked, cutting Liv off.

Her brow scrunched at the strange question. "A small hut."

The old woman shook her head. "No, look past that. What glamour do you see?"

"I see a few different ones," Liv explained.

Hawaiki set off, gathering wood from the ground. "And when you look at me, what form do I take?"

Liv scratched her head, trying to figure out how best to answer the question without sounding rude. She couldn't say, "You look like an old, saggy woman."

Studying the images shuffling in her head of the woman, Liv said, "Again, I see a few different ones. You young, and then older."

Hawaiki dropped wood by a firepit that hadn't been there a few moments prior. "Yes, that makes sense."

Liv had no idea how that made sense, but this was par for the course. "Hawaiki, I'm here because I need—"

"Help unlocking the memories your mother sealed into her sword," the elf said, interrupting her yet again.

Liv's mouth slammed shut with surprise, then she said, "Well, yes. How did you know?"

"First of all, I can sense your mother's sword, Inexorabilis, on you, and the memories are quite loud," Hawaiki explained. "Secondly, usually individuals see one particular image of my house, whichever one resonates with their own personal tastes. However, those who are lost can't see one form of my house, which means you need this information from your mother's sword unlocked to proceed on your path."

"Oh," Liv said, surprised by how accurate the old woman was with her observations.

"Well, and also, you look just like your mother," Hawaiki stated. "I knew you were Guinevere's daughter before you recognized me as a person."

"I was simply distracted," Liv stated. "And why can I see you at all ages?"

Hawaiki went to work arranging the wood. "That's a very good question, which I don't have the answer for at the present moment. Most see me in only one of my forms: child, teenager, adult, or elderly. You, Liv Beaufont, are a strange individual."

"Thank you?" Liv said, doubt in her voice.

A fire started with a flick of Hawaiki's fingers, lighting the dry kindling. "Now, why don't you come inside while this fire heats up. I'll serve you something to eat and take a look at this sword you've brought."

Liv nodded, following the old woman to the door. "That would be great."

Before Liv could enter, Hawaiki swung around with her hand out. "I can't have you dripping Rongo all over the place. Close your eyes, child. This might hurt a bit."

Liv tilted her head to the side, giving the old woman a skeptical expression.

With a frustrated look, Hawaiki said, "I've got to get you cleaned up. Or would you rather keep the bug guts in your ear canal and in between your ch—"

"Yes, yes," Liv said in a rush. "That's fine. Do it." She squeezed her eyes shut, wondering how getting cleaned could hurt. A moment later, she had her answer. It felt as though she'd had a squeegee raked over every inch of her body. Her ears, nose, and in between her toes felt like they'd been cleaned with pipe cleaners. And just when Liv thought it was done, a blast of wind knocked her back several feet, making her land in a dirt pile.

"Well, I cleaned you up once," Hawaiki said when Liv's eyes popped open. "You're on your own now."

Liv pushed to her feet, dusting off her backside. She was clean...well, mostly. The slime was gone, but she had some dirt on her jeans from her fall.

"Join me inside, would you?" Hawaiki said, disappearing into the hut.

Liv shook her head and followed her, hoping the house was bigger on the inside.

CHAPTER TWELVE

Not only was Hawaiki's house bigger on the inside, but it was also simply stunning. The floors were marble, with a swirling design of blues and greens. Overhead was a giant chandelier, and twin staircases framed the entryway. Through the living room, Liv could spy a sparkling pool, complete with a fountain and a gazebo.

"Wow, this isn't what I expected," Liv remarked, turning around completely to take in the beautiful craftsmanship of the home.

"You thought I'd have dirt floors, did you?"

Liv shook her head. "No. I mean, I wasn't sure what to expect. Maybe something a bit more modest. You do live on an island away from everyone."

"And I suppose that means I should drink well water and not have electricity?" Hawaiki asked.

Liv didn't know how to refute that. This was exactly what she had thought.

Hawaiki led Liv to a dining room table that sat beside a picture window that looked out on a giant waterfall, which she didn't remember seeing outside the hut. "It's okay. You're right to wonder," the elf confessed, guilt in her voice as she lowered her chin.

"I am?" Liv asked in disbelief.

"Yes," Hawaiki said. "I actually used to live in Manhattan. I had to have the trendiest clothes. If it was in, I wanted to be the first to get it. And the moment it was out, I tossed it in the trash." The old elven woman stared around. "This house is a mix of who I used to be. The outside and the place I've come to live, it reminds me of who I am. I can't live anymore in a world where I'm owned by what's popular and what isn't. I've given that up. However, I shouldn't suffer since I have grown to enjoy the conveniences of life, so I live away from others, enjoying a simple life. However, I still love my bamboo sheets and Juicy Couture handbags."

Liv was having a hard time trying to picture this island woman decked out in designer clothes and sporting a bag with a miniature dog hanging out of it. However, when her eyes weren't totally focused, she got brief glimpses of what Hawaiki had looked like years ago. She was in fact polished in her high heels, her hair slicked back in a bun, and her eyelash extensions batting as she gave disapproving looks to others.

"So was this other life of yours before or after you made my mother's sword?" Liv asked.

Hawaiki took a seat at the table, sighing loudly like she was relieved to get off her feet. "Oh, that was a long time before I went through my materialistic phase. I've gone through many evolutions, as I'm sure you will."

"I'm not sure you'll ever catch me wearing Prada," Liv remarked.

"Maybe not," Hawaiki mused. "But I'm sure you'll one day be a lover, a heartbreaker, a heartbreakee, a mother, a grandmother, an aunt, a friend, a betrayer, and many, many other things."

Liv didn't know what to say to that. She stood nervously in front of the table, her eyes shifting back and forth.

"You see, Liv Beaufont, we all have many different roles we play in life," Hawaiki stated. "I have never much cared for people, which is why you find me here. And at one point, I thought things could fill the void I'd created when I cut out the world. That didn't work, obviously. And so at this point, you find my incarnation here as an old woman who knows no one. There's no one for me to save or impress or expel."

"So before this, you were a socialite?" Liv asked, finding it hard to believe the woman she'd mistaken for a burlap sack had once been so into trends and fashion.

"Yes, and before I was the legendary sword maker, I was the one who colonized the Polynesian islands for my race," she explained. Hawaiki hummed, a bit of melancholy in her voice. "I think, like most, I've been trying to fill a void in my life with my achievements, power, possessions, and more. It's only now, in the last few chapters of my life, that I've tried to simplify things."

This wasn't the lesson Liv had expected, but it resonated with her in ways she'd also not anticipated.

Hawaiki tapped the table with her withered hands.

"Okay, let's see Inexorabilis. I haven't set eyes on one of my creations in a long, long time."

The excitement in Liv's chest blossomed until she thought she would explode. She couldn't believe she was here, and about to uncover her mother's final moments on Earth. So much had led up to this point. Liv wanted what would come next more than anything, and yet, she knew it would change everything. She might not like what she learned, and she was certain it would lead her on a new path with new challenges and dangers.

Liv pulled back her cape, taking her mother's sword from her hip. The electric shock that always accompanied touching Inexorabilis ran through her fingers, nearly making her drop it on the table.

Hawaiki leaned forward, spying Bellator on the other side of her. "Oh, you have two swords, do you? Guinevere's sword does not fit you, does it?"

"No. I already had this sword before finding my mother's," Liv explained, then amended, "And actually, no. The sword *doesn't* fit me. I've always, since I can remember, experienced a shock when I touched Inexorabilis."

"And you didn't believe this evidence that you could potentially be bonded to the sword?" she asked. "Some might have taken this as a positive sign."

Liv thought about it for a moment and shook her head. "No, it wasn't a magnetic shock. It was a repulsive one."

"Oh, like how you feel when you meet someone not right for you," Hawaiki guessed. "Not like the pulse you feel when you see a man you like."

Liv blushed. "I hadn't really thought of it that way, but yes."

"Do you know why I named this sword Inexorabilis?" Hawaiki asked.

Liv had a hundred guesses, but she wanted to hear the truth from the old sword maker. "Why?"

"Because your mother, Guinevere Beaufont, had a fire I'd rarely seen. You simply looked at your mother and thought, 'Wow, that woman is unstoppable.' I named the sword after her."

Liv took a seat, suddenly feeling heavy, although she wasn't sure why.

"Now, when I look at you, I see the same thing," Hawaiki continued. "So one might think that would make the sword perfect for you. But you aren't your mother. It is wrong for you to think you can fill her shoes as a Warrior for the House of Seven. She had her own role. Her own challenges. Her own achievements. You, Liv Beaufont, aren't meant to be a replica of your mother. You are meant to be your own thing. Therefore, I believe the sword has rejected you so that you become what you are meant to be, separate from what your mother blessed you with."

"So Inexorabilis rejected me?" Liv asked, her insides scorched slightly by the confirmation.

Hawaiki nodded, a sudden realization popping to her face. "Oh, dear. I said I'd feed you, and I haven't." She snapped her fingers, and two bowls appeared in front of them. They looked to be filled with broth and bones and strange leaves that gave off a pungent odor.

The old elf waved her hand forward, drawing in the scent from the soup with approval. "Oh, you'll enjoy this if you plug your nose and pretend its pizza."

Liv peered over the edge of the bowl. "Is that all I have to do?"

Hawaiki laughed, a strangely melodic sound. "Oh, yes. I'm a horrible cook, and the ingredients I have out here aren't ideal for making squat. I would apologize, but you *did* show up unannounced."

"Well, you don't have a telephone that I could have called on, right?" Liv asked.

"No, there's absolutely no way of getting in contact with me," Hawaiki said. "That's by design."

"Right." Liv pushed her soup away after taking a small whiff. "Thanks for this, but I'm not hungry."

"No, you just used a huge amount of magical power to cross lava and defeat a giant beetle." Hawaiki gave her a commiserating expression as she pushed her own bowl of soup away. "And yes, the sword rejected you because you're too much like your mother."

"I don't understand," Liv said, looking Inexorabilis over.

"It's a bit complex, but your mother's sword was created for her by me," Hawaiki explained. "It grew to know what she'd need. It anticipated her desires as a good sword does. It evolved with her. If you picked up this sword, then—"

"I'd have no evolution," Liv said, completing her sentence.

"That's exactly right," Hawaiki said triumphantly. "Instead, you had a sword made by a giant, which was created perfectly for you. I'm sure you've had your own trials and tribulations using that sword on your waist. If you'd had Inexorabilis, it wouldn't have given you what you wanted or needed since it already gave it to Guinevere."

Liv glanced down at Bellator, thinking of the journey they'd been on in the short time they'd been together. She wasn't about to argue about Bellator being giant-made. There was no point, she'd come to realize.

Everything Hawaiki had said about her mother's sword made sense. It had already gone through an orientation with Guinevere. They were so much alike, Liv and her mother. She didn't need her mother's sword because of that. It would offer her little. What she needed was her own sword, her own challenges, her own path as she took on the same role as her mother.

Pushing the sword over to Hawaiki, Liv held her breath. "Okay, I'm ready to find out what memories my mother's sword holds. Are you ready to tell me?"

The old elf considered this for a long moment, her wrinkled fingers resting on the hilt. "Yes, I'll tell you what you came here to find out. But please know—"

"That what I learn will change everything," Liv guessed. "My mother said as much in the last message she imbued into the blade."

Hawaiki shook her head. "There's that. And your mother was right to give you that warning, but there's something else."

Liv leaned forward, not breathing. "What else?"

"This is the last message your mother left," Hawaiki said, a coarseness to her voice. "It is the last remnants of your parents. Are you ready to see their final moments? To know their final wishes for their children? After this, the journey ahead will be all on your own. No more clues from your parents. It will be only you and your own to lead the way."

Liv thought about that. She'd silently felt her parents there with her on this journey, steering her with their clues and the wisdom they'd left behind. How many times had her father's hints whispered in her ears? How many times had her mother's lessons reminded her of what she needed to know? But this was the last thing they had left behind, and unearthing its secrets was like unburying them. Once that was done, there would be no more…

Liv would be on her own, fighting their war alone.

And then she remembered how else they had equipped her.

With Clark.

And Sophia.

With Rory.

And Rudolf.

With Stefan.

And then there were John and Plato, and so many others. Whether her parents had meant her to have so many friends or not didn't matter. She had them now. And she was ready to face whatever came next, even if that meant hearing her parent's last messages and therefore letting go of everything they had left behind.

"I'm ready," she said to Hawaiki, pushing Inexorabilis toward the elf, feeling the shock radiate in her fingers.

## CHAPTER THIRTEEN

With a meditative expression, Hawaiki pulled Inexorabilis closer to her. She ran her hands an inch over the blade, her eyes starting to glaze over as she chanted in a soft whisper. Liv realized after a minute that she was holding her breath, the anticipation in her chest ready to bound out of her.

The elf's eyelids fluttered shut and her head lolled back like she was falling asleep. Worried that she had actually nodded off, Liv considered interrupting her.

And then the sword began to rise off the surface of the table and glow. A strange chiming noise resonated from the blade, making it vibrate. Mesmerized by this show, Liv watched unblinking until the sword clattered back to the table as Hawaiki pulled her hands to her sides like she'd been burned. Her brown eyes were wide with shock.

"What was it?" Liv asked, leaning forward. "Is everything okay?"

Hawaiki stood abruptly, shaking her head at Inexorabilis. "You shouldn't have brought this sword here."

Liv copied her, standing and pushing the seat out behind her. "What? Why? What did you see?"

The old elf continued to shake her head. "You've put me in great danger. I know things I shouldn't know."

"The Mortal Seven?" Liv asked.

Hawaiki stumbled backward, stabilizing herself on the wall. "Your parents were trying to uncover a secret."

"Yes, mortals used to be able to see magic," Liv said, trying to keep her voice calm, although the older woman was visibly shaking.

"And they made many enemies because of their pursuit of justice."

"Yes. Did you see who murdered them?" Liv asked.

Hawaiki gulped, her eyes still wide with shock. "Yes," she said in a hushed voice.

"Who was it?" Liv's voice was shaking.

"They were trying to shut off a signal on the top of the Matterhorn," Hawaiki said carefully.

"Yes, the one that keeps mortals from seeing magic."

"You already know they were killed climbing that mountain, don't you?" Hawaiki asked.

"Yes." Liv nearly yelled. This exchange was happening too slowly. She needed answers right now. "It wasn't an accident, was it?"

Hawaiki shook her head. "They were tricked."

"How?" Liv asked.

Carefully, Hawaiki took a step forward. "Your mother left a message in the sword. It would be best if you heard it from her."

Liv didn't know what to do. Her eyes shifted back and forth uncertainly. "Do I touch Inexorabilis?"

Hawaiki nodded. "Yes, and once you're done, I must ask that you do something for me."

Liv blinked at the old woman. "What?"

"I need you to wipe my memory," she answered.

"What? Really? Why?" Liv asked.

The elf shook her head. "You'll have to see what your mother left for you first." She wrung her hands, indecision heavy in her eyes. "I wished I could help, but this is too big. I need to live a quiet life. I can't remember what I now know."

"Okay." Liv reached across the table, her fingers falling on Inexorabilis. The shock was almost startling this time, making Liv gasp from the sensation. Her eyes shut at once without her permission. Like when she entered the Door of Reflection, she was instantly in a dreamscape.

She stood on the ridge of the Matterhorn, the wind sweeping through her hair. Liv searched the area, wondering why she was there. Her hand went straight for Bellator, but it wasn't there. She felt naked without her sword. Defenseless. But why should she need a weapon? This was only a dream.

Doing a full turn, Liv tried to understand why she was there. Where was the message her mother had left for her? She recognized the area where she stood. It looked similar to where she'd found Inexorabilis. Where her parents had died.

"If you're here, you've learned the tragic truth," Guinevere Beaufont said, her voice at Liv's back.

She tensed. Pressed her eyes shut. This wasn't real. She knew that. But nothing had ever felt more real in all her life.

Bracing herself, Liv turned to face the image of her mother. She, like Liv, was solid. Her mother looked exactly as she remembered, with her long flowing blonde hair and her kind blue eyes. She regarded her daughter with a tender smile, her chin held high.

"Mommy…" Liv didn't recognize her own voice. She sounded like a child again.

"My sweet Olivia," her mother said, holding out her arms to her.

Without hesitation, Liv raced forward, throwing her arms around her mother. And to her astonishment, Guinevere's form felt solid. She squeezed her daughter to her. It was as if the last five years hadn't happened. Liv had never left. She'd never missed her parents. She'd never felt the loneliness that had filled her after leaving the House of Seven. She had never locked her magic and given up her birthright.

In this reality, there had been a happy ending for the Beaufont family.

However, Liv knew that wasn't what had really happened.

She pulled back from her mother, astonishment on her face. "How are you here?"

"Oh, look at how you've grown, my child. You're more beautiful than I ever could have imagined." Her eyes ran over Liv as she gave an appreciative smile. "You're strong and healthy. I'm grateful for that. But are you happy, Olivia?"

Liv wanted to launch straight into things, sharing everything with her mother. But she couldn't get over the fact that she was there.

"Mommy, how are you here? I don't understand."

Guinevere smiled thoughtfully at her daughter. "I froze a portion of my spirit into Inexorabilis in case my children should ever find the sword and need answers."

"But how?" Liv asked, knowing that doing something of that nature was incredibly difficult. She'd never heard of anyone accomplishing such a thing.

"I sacrificed whatever would have come next, after my death," Guinevere explained. "I chose to live in a purgatory of sorts, at least for now—until one of my children found me."

"But does that mean you've stayed stuck here on Earth?"

She nodded.

"And Daddy?" Liv asked.

"He moved on," her mother explained.

"But you left a part of your spirit in the sword? Why?" Liv asked.

"Because I didn't want to leave my children," Guinevere explained, then shook her head. "Of course, I wouldn't want to leave you. But I knew if something happened to me, I had to leave you with answers. It was important to me that this family of Beaufonts ended things once and for all."

"I don't understand," Liv said, none of this computing.

Her mother nodded. "I knew if something took me from this world, it would also come after my children. I couldn't leave you all defenseless."

"So before you died, you put this piece of your soul into the sword?" Liv asked, shocked at the amount of power her mother would have had to harness to do such a thing.

She'd never heard of anyone else being able to do anything like that.

"We don't have much time. I'm sorry to rush, but I have to tell you things quickly." Her mother pointed to the summit of the Matterhorn. "Olivia, you know what is up there, don't you?"

She nodded. "There's a signal that prevents mortals from seeing magic."

Appreciatively, her mother nodded. "I suspected that our children would follow the clues we left behind. Ian and Reese have been investigating this, I suspect."

Liv froze. She didn't know how to tell her mother the truth about her children, even the spirit of her mother. How could she relay to her that two of her children were dead? This wasn't how she'd pictured this impossible reunion going.

But Liv's face must have given it away.

"They were killed, weren't they?" Guinevere asked.

"I'm sorry," Liv said in reply. The expression her mother gave her in reply weakened her knees. Never before had she seen heartbreak like this on anyone's face.

Guinevere wiped a single tear from the corner of her eye and stood up straighter. "I never meant to put my children in danger, but I also know that we, the Beaufonts, do not live a life without hazards. We have inherited an important legacy, and unfortunately, I knew my children would face these challenges."

"Legacy?" Liv asked. "You mean as Warriors and Councilors for the House?"

Her mother shook her head. "That's part of it, but it's not why you are here."

"Why am I here?" Liv asked, feeling like the question was strange as it tumbled out of her mouth.

"Olivia, you know about the Great War, right?"

"Yes, against mortals and magicians," she answered.

"That's right," Guinevere said. "The Beaufonts were against the war. Your father's family didn't think the two sides should battle. However, there was so much tension between the two forces that the Beaufonts couldn't stop it. What happened after the war constructed much of the world the way you experience it presently. I don't know everything that happened because much of it was covered up."

"Like how the history was erased and retold?" Liv inquired.

"Yes. I see you've been hard at work, finding the truth." Guinevere stared at the summit for a long moment before continuing, "After the war, the Warrior and the Councilor for the Beaufont family created an incredibly powerful spell in secret. They made it so that no matter what, we as Beaufonts would always be able to find the truth."

"What?" Liv asked, already knowing the answer. "That mortals can see magic?" Then remembering what Papa Creola had said, she added, "That mortals are the source of magic?"

Guinevere's blue eyes lit up. "You are even more bright than when I left you, my dear."

Liv blushed. It felt strange to hear this from her mother, and yet, it was one of the many compliments she'd longed for over the last five years. Being smart without her mother to witness it hadn't been enough. Being brave without her father to appreciate it had been insufficient.

To stand there and have her mother's spirit appreciate her...well, it went far to mend some of the broken pieces.

"You see, my darling, a lot happened in the aftermath of the war," Guinevere explained. "But your father's ancestors, knowing things were about to change forever, created a spell so that a Beaufont would always search out the truth, and, one day, hopefully, uncover it."

"So we are compelled to discover the secrets about mortals?" Liv asked.

Her mother nodded. "It's our role in the House, or at least one of them."

Liv didn't know what to do with this information. It slightly made her deflate as she realized she wasn't special for deciphering the clues Reese and Ian left behind. She was only treading the path the spell had set her on.

"For generations," her mother continued, "Beaufonts have been trying to uncover the truth about mortals. However, something or rather someone has always stopped us."

"Do you know who?" Liv asked.

"I do now," Guinevere answered. "However, before my death, I did not. And those who came before your father and me, they didn't know. There are those who are bent on keeping the secret, in keeping mortals away from the House, and therefore keeping magic hidden from mortals. And then there are those whose job it is to fix things, making the world the way it was before."

"The Beaufonts," Liv said, realizing the legacy she'd inherited.

"Yes, my child," her mother stated. "Only a Beaufont can relay the secret regarding mortals. The spell set up long ago makes it so that if anyone else shares the truth, they'll forget it almost at once unless it is specifically told to them by a Beaufont. However, if they are informed by a Beaufont, then not only will they not forget it, but they will feel the urge to fix things back to how they were."

"So you're saying that if Bob Johnson or Jim Smith or whoever knows about the mortals' secret history, they will soon forget it," Liv said slowly, trying to wrap her mind around this complexity. "However, if they are informed by a Beaufont, then not only can they not forget it, but they will want to fix things?"

The way her mother's face transformed when she laughed nearly took Liv's breath away. "Yes. I've missed your humor, Olivia."

Again, Liv blushed. "Then why wouldn't our family just make a huge announcement so that mortals came back?"

Guinevere nodded, a knowing look in her eyes. "Generations ago, one of your ancestors tried that. Everyone they told was killed. You see, knowing the truth doesn't make us invincible. Quite the opposite. We are targets. Searching for the truth puts a bullseye on our backs, as I'm sure you've discovered.

"Unfortunately, there are no history books about the Beaufonts or those in the House of Seven for you to study. If there were, you'd find that every single generation of Warrior and Councilor in our family has met an untimely death. This wasn't a role your father and I took on lightly after hearing the truth. However, you know the hidden history, and would you back down from this mission?"

"Absolutely not!" Liv said with unexpected passion. "We

need mortals. They need us. If I don't connect them back to magic, then—"

"Then we will lose it forever," her mother finished her sentence. "That was exactly why your father and I worked so hard to fulfill what his ancestors had tirelessly tried to uncover time and time again. But in the end, we obviously failed."

"No, Mommy," Liv argued. "You left behind clues. The Warrior's ring and Inexorabilis and more."

"Your father and I knew the risks we faced, and we knew it was worth it. We couldn't raise our family and not fight for your future at the same time. And as you now realize, a Beaufont is compelled to uncover the truth. That's how the spell operates. And since only those informed by a Beaufont will remember the secret, we only ever told one other person."

"Bermuda Laurens," Liv said in a whisper, guessing.

"Yes, and although she tried to help us, the dangers and risks became too much for her," Guinevere explained. "Before our deaths, she quit pursuing the truth."

Liv smiled slightly. "Bermuda is back on the case now."

Guinevere returned the grin. "I'm not surprised. Even if one abandons the mission for a little while, it won't last. The spell makes it so they are restless if they aren't searching for and uncovering the truth about mortals. That's how strong the spell your ancestors put on their family long ago was."

"But why?" Liv asked.

"Without us, the secret regarding mortals would stay buried forever. History was erased and changed. Mortals can't see magic. There is little reason to question things, based on how they were covered up. But there is one and only one family who will always remember the truth and seek to uncover it. That's us, my darling. The Beaufonts are the only way that things will ever change, return to normal. Even the Mortal Seven don't have the power to change things. They are stuck in the history as it was rewritten."

"But Bermuda met an elf who knew the truth because he'd been around since the beginning of time or something," Liv recounted, thinking of the ancient elf Bermuda had questioned when trying to find out how history was erased.

"There are a few who know the truth, like Papa Creola," Guinevere explained. "But even fae who have been around since the Great War can't remember how things were. Only those who have been cut off from society for so long that their memory is untampered with. And still, one elf can't change things."

"Yes, but I'm only one person too," Liv argued. "Clark and Sophia and I, we are just—"

Guinevere reached out and grabbed her daughter's hand. "You are all we have left, my child. If something happens to you three, the history will die with you. Mortals can't save themselves from this. There are no other magical families under the same spell as you. Only the Beaufonts have the power to change things."

"I've been trying, Mommy," Liv stated, gripping her mother's hand tightly.

"I know, and if you're here, then you've done a remarkable job. I daresay you've made it farther than anyone else."

"Yes, but every Beaufont has died trying to uncover the

truth. What chance do I have?" Liv asked, suddenly feeling defeated.

"You have a rare chance that no one before you has had." Guinevere pointed to the rocks in the distance and Liv noticed Inexorabilis poking out of the rubble, exactly the way it had been when she recovered it. "Leaving behind information for the next generation has been difficult. Those who don't want the secret out there, who are as adamant about protecting it as we are driven to uncover it, have never stopped destroying anything we left behind. They've killed to stop us from investigating. They've taken our property, so there was nothing for our children to learn from. However, you found Inexorabilis, and therefore, you have a unique advantage that no others have had."

"Because you sealed a part of yourself into the sword?" Liv asked.

Her mother nodded. "That means I can tell you something that will give you an advantage few have ever had."

Liv tensed. Prepared herself. "Yes."

"My sweet Olivia, you must find a way to unregister your magic."

Of all the things Liv expected her mother to say, this wasn't it. "What? Why?"

"Since this has been going on, the Royals from the House have had their magic registered," Guinevere explained. "Your father and I were killed, much the same way as I suspect Ian and Reese were, and how I believe now that your ancestors were murdered."

"I don't understand why unregistering my magic will change anything," Liv stated. And not only that, she had no idea how to unregister her magic in the first place. She was a Warrior for the House of Seven. If they couldn't follow her magic, it would be discovered immediately.

"The day your father and I were murdered, we tried to fight, but we never stood a chance."

"Because your magic had been locked," Liv guessed.

Her mother nodded. "That's right. As long as your magic is registered, you'll be at a disadvantage when you stand against the one who has taken us down for generations."

*Of course,* Liv thought. If the Beaufonts were the family who was charged with uncovering the secrets, there had to be one who had the opposite mission.

"Mommy, who murdered you?" Liv asked, already knowing the answer but needing to hear it.

Her mother smiled serenely at her. "It was Adler Sinclair. He locked our magic and then used his power to push us to our deaths."

## CHAPTER FOURTEEN

At her core, Liv had known this.

Adler Sinclair had killed her family.

She'd known her parents had been murdered. Deep down, she'd suspected that it had been covered up by the House of Seven. And her innate dislike of Adler told her he was a bad guy. But she had to admit she hadn't known he'd been the one to kill her parents, not really. It made sense, yes, but not until faced with the startling truth could she really digest this as a fact.

"He killed you," Liv said with a gasp. "With your magic locked, he stood up here and struck you down like some coward."

Guinevere nodded. "So now you see why you must have your magic unregistered. You, Clark, and Sophia." Her mother's expression shifted suddenly. "Oh, how are they? Is Clark pushing himself as hard as usual? And little Sophia? Is she growing up strong?"

For what felt like a too short of a period of time, Liv and her mother spoke on the path up to the Matterhorn. It was surreal for Liv. Strange and spooky. Perfect, and also not quite right. She wanted the reunion to be somewhere else. A place that wasn't only feet from the place of her parents' death. And yet, this was all she had, and it was over before she was ready.

"My love," Guinevere interrupted when Liv was telling her about Sophia. "I'm sorry, but I have to go."

"I don't want you to," Liv said, her tears close to the surface.

"I know, but my time is up. I can't stay here much longer."

Liv's eyes darted to Inexorabilis. "Are you going back into the sword?"

She shook her head. "Oh, no. You freed me, darling. I have no reason to return there. One of my children found me, as I intended. Now I finally get to move on."

The tears Liv had been holding back from the beginning tried to force their way to the surface. "Will you go on to see Daddy?"

Guinevere's blue eyes watered. "I really don't know, my love."

"If you do, will you tell him—"

Her mother held up her hand, silencing her. "He knows you love him. There is no one who has felt the warmth of your love and not known how you felt about them, because when you care about someone, it's like sunshine on a cool day, Olivia. But if I get to see your father again, I'd like to tell him something that he doesn't know. That I don't know. Something only you can answer for us."

Liv blinked at her mother, wondering what this grand question would be. "Yes?"

"Olivia, are you happy?" Guinevere asked.

It was such a simple question. The simplest, really—either yes or no. That was the answer. It was like asking whether someone was hot or cold. It wasn't complex. And yet, Liv stalled, not knowing how to answer her mother's question.

"I'm close," she finally said.

Her mother, who was still holding her hand, squeezed it with a beautiful force that constricted Liv's heart. "What's holding you back, my love?"

"It's just that I miss you both so much. And then there's Ian and Reese, and…" The tears came now, pouring down Liv's cheeks, reminding her that she was a girl with hurts and fears and a history of spells from her ancestors and not just a magician who was impenetrable, as she often thought.

"You don't have to give up happiness for us," Guinevere said. "If anything, we died so that one day, the next generation could get that much closer to the truth. To a place where all races are happy. And you aren't excluded from that, my dear. You might be a Warrior for the House, but your right to happiness is the same as everyone else's. It is your birthright. You were born to find the truth. You were born to fight for justice. And more than anything, Olivia Beaufont, you were born to be happy."

CHAPTER FIFTEEN

Liv's mother began to fade too soon. They barely had time to hug and cry in each other's arms before Liv was back in Hawaiki's kitchen, her present reality spiraling away around her.

"She told you the truth?" the old elf asked when Liv opened her eyes, her fingers still pressed into Inexorabilis.

Liv kept her fingers there, thinking she might be transported to the Matterhorn. She just needed one more glimpse of her mother's timeless eyes and carefree smile. She just needed to cement her image in her mind so that one day, when she was old, she could remember the person who had inspired her the most with her passion and courage.

When the sword didn't transport her, Liv glanced at the elf, shaking her head. "Is she…"

"She's gone," Hawaiki answered. "She stayed for as long as she intended."

"But I had more to say to her," Liv argued as if this had been Hawaiki's doing.

"There is never enough time for two tethered souls on Earth."

"But—"

"What your mother did is something I've never seen," Hawaiki said, cutting her off. "She sacrificed a great deal to relay that information to you. To take that chance. You might have never found her sword, and then she'd be stuck forever. That was the risk she took. You must always be grateful that you had the time you did with her. This was truly a gift that most never have with those they've lost."

Liv nodded, realizing the old elf was right. She'd seen her mother one last time, something she'd never thought possible. Pulling her hand away from her mother's sword, she straightened, trying to compose herself.

"So you want me to erase your memory because you don't want to take up this crusade," Liv guessed.

Hawaiki's face was covered with shame. "I realize that I should help, but my time fighting battles is over. I'd like to live out the rest of my life in peace."

Liv couldn't argue with that. If she'd ever been given a choice, she might choose to not know the truth. However, she suspected she wouldn't. Fighting for justice was something that ran deep in her blood. She knew that now. Her ancestors had done everything so that she could stop the tyranny that had started long ago, and Liv didn't want to rest until she put an end to what her mother and her father and her ancestors had fought against.

"I understand," Liv said, stepping around the table. "What all would you like me to erase?"

"Just the memories in the sword," Hawaiki answered. "I'd like to remember you and our short time together. But just tell me that I didn't need to know the rest. I think I'll understand that."

Liv nodded, holding up her hand and focusing. A moment later, the spell was done.

Hawaiki blinked at Liv as if trying to orient herself and then glanced around. "We did it?"

"Yes," Liv answered, picking up Inexorabilis and sheathing it.

"I asked you to wipe my memory, did I?" Hawaiki asked.

"You didn't want to know the rest," Liv answered.

The old woman nodded. "I can't argue with my past self. It knows what I want for my future, which is mostly relaxation and honest hard work."

"And I hope that's all that's in store for you, Hawaiki."

The elf appeared like she wanted to say something. She opened her mouth several times, but nothing ever came out. "I guess I should show you the way out."

Liv nodded, feeling heavy with emotions.

When they exited the house, Liv blinked from the bright light in the jungle and the strange surroundings she'd forgotten about. It felt like a few years since she had stood outside the mud hut and staring at the jungle in the distance.

"I hope you got what you were looking for, Liv Beaufont," Hawaiki said, halting when she came to the roaring fire she'd built.

"I'm not sure I know what I came here for, but I got more than I was expecting."

"And now, when you look at my home, what do you see?" Hawaiki asked.

Liv focused on the mud hut for a moment and noticed that it transformed into a beautiful white house with a large tree out front. "I see a home. A real one."

With a knowing smile, Hawaiki nodded. "Yes, as I suspected."

"What did you suspect?"

"Whatever I showed you in your mother's sword, it healed a part of your spirit that was holding you back," she answered. "You aren't lost, as you were before."

Liv didn't know what to make of that. She stared mesmerized at the beautiful home for a long while before directing her gaze to Hawaiki. The elf still took on different forms of herself: a child, a teenager, an adult, and an elderly woman.

"I still see you in all your incarnations, though," Liv stated.

"Oh, yes," Hawaiki said. "I didn't expect that to change."

"Why?"

"Because there's something unique about you, Liv Beaufont. You don't see the world the same as others, which is why you don't see me in one of my forms but rather all of them. I'm not sure what you saw in your mother's sword or where you'll go from here, but I suspect that what lies ahead on your journey will touch the world. Only someone who can see things in such a holistic way can actually change the broken bits on this sphere we call home."

Liv didn't know what to say to that. She was about to nod and simply say thank you when a noise caught her attention.

Tensing, Liv glanced up to find Indikos sitting dangerously close to the fire.

Unstartled by the miniature dragon's sudden arrival, Hawaiki glanced affectionately at Indikos.

With a proud smile, she said to Liv, "I think I won his favor."

"With the fire?" Liv guessed.

She shook her head. "Oh, no. The fire was only a house-warming present."

Liv laughed, grateful to find someone else who enjoyed puns.

"Indikos came out of hiding because he has decided to give me a chance," Hawaiki explained. "And from here on out, all we can do is get to know each other and see if things work out."

Liv thought of the simplicity of the statement. Wasn't that what most were trying to do? Spend time together to figure out if things were going to work? If they didn't, that was when the real work began.

Pulling the herb Rory had given her from her pocket, Liv carefully unwrapped it. Then she took a small bite of the leaf and chewed. A moment later, she heard a voice in her head that she knew wasn't hers.

*I like her,* Indikos said. *I like it here, and I'd like to stay.*

Liv nodded appreciatively. *I'm glad. I hope you find happiness here.*

The miniature dragon flapped his wings and took off for the sky, soaring freely. *I hope the same for you, Liv Beaufont. Thank you for all that you've done to free me.*

CHAPTER SIXTEEN

Akio stumbled back when Liv threw a punch into the pad he'd been holding up. He gave her a look of surprise, not accustomed to her throwing him off balance during their sparring matches. There were few fighters as strong and resilient as Akio Takahashi.

He lowered the target he'd been holding. "A sleeping dragon has awoken within you."

Liv blinked at him in confusion before realizing this was another of the metaphors he threw out during their practices. She couldn't tell him the truth about Adler. And what was worse was, now she realized she couldn't tell him or anyone else the truth about mortals without signing them up for the crusade. It wasn't like she'd been volunteering the information before, but now it felt much more like an obligation to keep secret.

Still, she wondered how the Sinclairs and the Beaufonts had found their respective roles in the House and the Takahashis had managed to stay out of it. She silently wished she could have been a Takahashi. However, if she were honest with herself, Liv knew that was only good in theory. At her core, she believed she was a Beaufont because she was a person who wanted justice. She was proud that she was part of a family who had made sacrifices through the generations for a future of peace. She wouldn't be content in any other family. Besides, the Takahashis had their own hardships, and whatever they were, she was sure they were unique to them.

Shaking off the adrenaline, Liv said, "I think more than just a dozing dragon has awoken inside me."

Akio regarded her for a long moment, studying her in that way that was unique to him, where he seemed to peer into her soul. "Confronting our enemies never heals what they did that wronged us."

Liv had been fantasying about what she'd do to Adler when she found him. She'd played through a hundred different scenarios. He was the one who had murdered her parents and Ian and Reese. He was going to pay. She didn't know where he was or when he'd turn up, but when they came face to face, whether it was in the House of Seven or somewhere else, she'd make him suffer.

But Akio was right. Whatever she did to Adler wasn't going to bring back her family. It might make her feel marginally better, but she was wrong to think it would fix anything. All it would do was take a bad man from this place so she could change what he'd done to the magical world. That was a start, but it wasn't healing. That was something she could only give herself.

Liv was about to regroup so they could continue when Akio straightened, bowing to someone standing in the door of the studio.

"Little Rider, have you come to join us?" Akio asked.

Turning, Liv found Sophia. She wore a pale blue dress, and had a light scarf tied around her neck and a floppy hat on her head. "I'm sorry, Master Takahashi. Not today. I only interrupt because my sister has an appointment I need to take her to."

Liv's brow scrunched as she regarded her little sister. "Appointment?"

Sophia nodded, tapping her wrist. "And we'll be late unless you hurry up and get ready. This has been booked for ages."

Liv wiped the sweat from her head, trying to remember what appointment she had. Then it hit her, and she remembered exactly why she'd forgotten.

Sighing, Liv turned to Akio and bowed. "I would rather stay and have you kick my butt for several more hours than go do what I must."

He returned the bow with a slight smile. "I don't believe I was the one with the victorious edge this round, but may I offer you some advice, Warrior Beaufont?"

"Always," she said, realizing she'd come to think of Akio as a friend. It was strange because when she'd entered the House of Seven, she hadn't wanted any help, and now she realized the valuable talents of those all around her whom she'd at first judged to be elitist. It just proved that not everyone in the House was bad. The Sinclairs were, and there had to be others. It would be part of Liv's mission to find all those and punish them, along with Adler and Decar. That was part of her role in justice.

"If you lose yourself saving the world, will it really be worth it?" Akio asked her.

She opened her mouth, thinking the answer was easy. But all of a sudden it wasn't. Her original answer of "Yes, absolutely" didn't seem right. Would her parents be proud of her if she finished what they started but forgot who she was?

Liv simply nodded to her friend. "Thank you. I'll take that under advisement."

"I'm certain you will," Akio said. "You're a smart and skillful Warrior. Don't allow your anger to color what you know to be true in your heart."

***

"Seriously, you had to come and get me for this appointment?" Liv asked, trying to stay completely still so she didn't get stuck with a pin yet again.

"Yes," Sophia said, lying on her stomach and thumbing through a book. "King Rudolf sent sixteen messages to your place when you didn't show up."

Liv sighed, catching the seamstress' annoyed expression. She hadn't been the best model, not staying still during her fitting. But also wearing a tight-fitting formal gown of pink and neon green also wasn't her ideal circumstance. However, as the best man for Rudolf's wedding, she was expected to match the groomsmen, who would be wearing suits in the couple's colors.

"I'm going to need you to suck in, honey," the seamstress said, lacing fabric around Liv's waist.

"I think I'd rather not."

Sophia glanced up, giggling. "I think you're going to

look like a princess. That's one of the most amazing dresses I've ever seen."

Liv had to admit that she was right. The material had been spelled so that it shifted colors alternating between pink and green. Flowers were supposed to bloom on the dress in places, depending on the wearer's mood. It also gave off the scent of springtime, making Liv strangely feel light even with all the frustrating thoughts rolling around inside her brain.

Desperately she wanted to tell Sophia about what she'd learned about Adler and their magic, but she didn't know how. It was a weight she didn't want to place on the young girl's shoulders. Thankfully, Sophia didn't have her magic registered yet, so they didn't have to worry about fixing that. But for her and Clark, it was a different story, and a whole lot more complicated.

A wisp of smoke shot out of Liv's bag, which was lying in the corner. Sophia and Liv exchanged other wide-eyed expressions that said, "What in the world was that?" However, the seamstress didn't seem to notice.

"What was that?" Sophia asked.

Liv tried to remember what all was in her bag. Then she remembered the anywhere pad Rory had given her. Thinking it was safe for Sophia to check out and unable to move, she encouraged her to take a look for her.

After rummaging through the bag, Sophia held up the anywhere pad, which simply said, "I'm with Mum. We're safe…for now."

## CHAPTER SEVENTEEN

Out on Roya Lane, Liv was grateful to be back in her regular clothes with a bit of sunlight kissing the top of her head. She kept Sophia close to her as they navigated the busy street.

She was grateful Rory and Bermuda were safe, but thinking that Decar was after them was unnerving. And now she knew that they were set on this mission because of her, because of her parents. If something happened to them, it would be her fault. Then she'd really be out for vengeance.

Liv tried to remember what Akio had told her: saving the world wasn't worth it if she lost herself. Which meant it wasn't enough to fix things. She had to fix things the right way. Which probably meant the hard way.

"Can we go into this shop?" Sophia asked, dragging Liv into a store that had strange toys and books. The building blocks stacked on each other, creating different structures depending on who was playing the game. The books projected scenes, creating dazzling visions in midair. And the child who played with the dollhouses could shrink down and become an actual character in the tiny homes.

Liv and her sister explored Roya Lane for hours. It was a leisurely afternoon, and Liv had rarely allowed herself those. However, after everything she'd been through, she knew her spirit needed this. There would be time to fight. There would be a chance to fix things. Right then, though, she needed time with Sophia, the person who grounded her the most.

"Oh, what do you think about this for a wedding present for Rudolf and Serena?" Sophia asked, holding up a pair of self-brushing toothbrushes.

"Good idea, but I don't think the fae have to brush their teeth," Liv stated. "I think they magically have no plaque and pleasant breath."

"What about Serena?" Sophia asked.

"I don't think she knows to brush her teeth. She hasn't gotten there yet."

Sophia snickered and picked up a frying pan. On the inside, it said, "For sunny side up." On the bottom, it read, "For knocking him upside the head."

"What about this?" she asked Liv

"You know what? I think that's absolutely perfect for the happy couple." She directed Sophia to the cash register for the store, where she was surprised to find Subner seemingly waiting for her, a sour expression on his face as usual.

"Hey," Liv said, looking at him cautiously. "Does you-know-who have a mission for me?"

He shook his head. "But he wants you to stop by and see him."

Liv nodded as she requested that the frying pan be gift-wrapped.

---

"Why do you think that Papa Creola requested you?" Sophia asked as they strode to the far end of the lane.

Liv shrugged. "I don't know what's going through that little man's head half the time."

"Do you think he'll mind that I'm with you?" Sophia asked.

"No. If he requested that I show up, then he knows you're with me." Liv pointed toward The Fantastical Armory. "The man knows what's going to happen before it happens, which probably makes most dinner parties and magic shows pretty boring for him."

Sophia laughed. "Do you really think Father Time goes to magic shows?"

Before Liv could answer, Papa Creola waved them in from the front step. "Get in here, already. I've been waiting for you forever."

Liv gave the gnome a look of disbelief. "Seriously, forever? Are you sure you're not being a bit melodramatic?"

"No, I'm not," he said, more on edge than usual.

"And really, shouldn't have you known exactly when to expect us?" Liv asked.

"Just because I know most things doesn't mean I know everything, Liv," he said to her before giving his attention to Sophia. "And to answer your question, I attend as many children's birthday parties as I can, although incognito. I actually enjoy the magic acts, but your sister wouldn't believe it."

Sophia offered her hand to the gnome. "It's a pleasure to meet you."

Papa Creola, who was the same height as the little girl, wrung her glove-covered hand. "The pleasure is all mine, Sophia Beaufont." When their hands met, he closed his eyes, an odd smile on his face. "Oh, yes, you have a strange and assorted future that not even I can influence. What an interesting life."

"Pops?" Liv asked. "What's going on?"

His eyes snapped open. "Right. Sorry. It's not every day that I meet Sophia Beaufont."

Liv gave her sister a sideways look full of caution. "Is everything okay?"

"Yes, as long as you're working on that thing so magic isn't erased forever," Papa Creola said, leading them farther into the shop, where there was actually a crowd of people.

"I think you know I am," Liv replied. "I could devote more time to it, but I'm supposed to go to this wedding… unless you think I should be excused from it for official Father Time business."

He shook his head. "Oh, no. I'll actually be in attendance as well. A wedding is a holy affair. And you especially should be there. It's important for…well, future events."

Liv gave Sophia another sideways look. "Isn't it cute how he alludes to knowing things about my life but won't say anything specific?"

"It's adorable," said Papa Creola and Sophia at the same time, one of them meaning it and the other not.

Her mouth popped open with surprise, but the gnome simply winked. "The bathroom is in the back, and yes, I'll have you two out of here in just a few minutes. Way before your dragon wakes up from his nap in his shell."

Sophia's eyes widened in disbelief.

Liv leveled her gaze at her sister. "See, it's freaking cute, isn't it? Try planning a surprise party for the guy. It's annoying."

With an uncomfortable laugh, Sophia curtsied and dismissed herself, heading to the bathroom.

"Why would you throw me a surprise party?" Papa Creola asked Liv.

"For your birthday, of course," she answered.

"Which is?" he asked, sounding amused.

"January first," she guessed.

"Nice try," he said, leading her to the back, where there were a few elves and other magical creatures gathered. "I brought you here so you could help with the selection process."

"Selection process?" Liv asked.

"Well, how am I supposed to attend weddings or help with other things if I don't have employees in the place?" he asked.

"So you're actually expanding?" Liv questioned, surprised.

"Liv, I told you I was back and would employ others to filter requests and be the first line of defense," he explained.

"So does that mean you'll need my help less?" Liv asked.

He shook his head. "No. After what you accomplished

at Hawaiki's place, I think you've sealed the top position in my office."

"What I accomplished?"

"Did you see the elf as young or old?" he asked, a mischievous grin on his face.

She shook her head. "I saw her in all her ages."

He nodded proudly. "Which makes you the perfect employee for Father Time. You see people as timeless because you aren't as governed by the restraints of time."

"I have no idea what that means," she said.

"I know," he said, handing her a simple clipboard. "But one day, you will."

"What do I do with this?" she asked, indicating the clipboard.

"Go filter out the bad employees," he said, ushering her forward.

"So I should find the ones who will make your job easier?" she asked, studying the questionnaire on the page. There were questions like, "When traveling between point A and B, what's the fastest way to bypass and get to M?"

Papa Creola shook his head. "Oh, no. I invited you to help with hiring because having the right people will make *your* job easier. You've been promoted."

"Because I saw all the ages of Hawaiki?" Liv asked in disbelief.

"There was that. But also because when you learned the truth, you didn't overreact."

Liv thought about that for a moment. "I thought you knew what was going to happen before it happened. If so, didn't you know I wouldn't overreact or that I'd see all ages of Hawaiki?"

Papa Creola held up a finger, pausing her. "There is the magic in life for me. I see potentials. Very real possibilities. However, you, Liv Beaufont, continue to do things I don't suspect."

"Shouldn't that make me a risk?" she dared to ask.

He shrugged. "It also makes you highly entertaining, which is something I need after a few centuries of boredom," he said, encouraging her toward the group of magical creatures vying for jobs with Father Time.

## CHAPTER EIGHTEEN

"Are you sure about this?" Clark asked, looking cautiously at Liv as they stood outside the Chamber of the Tree.

Liv gave him a meaningful look and nodded.

She hadn't liked seeing the hurt expression on her brother's face when she'd told him what happened with their mother. He was jealous. How could he not be? She would have been too if he'd had one last moment with their mother without her. But it wasn't like she had known it was going to happen.

Thinking back, there were a hundred things she'd wished she'd told their mother when she had the chance. It had all happened so fast, and so much had transpired in a matter of minutes, then Guinevere Beaufont was gone. Stardust and ash, floating away in the wind.

In a place they knew to be safe, Liv told her brother what their mother had told her about unregistering her magic. At first, Clark was against it, but when she told him how their parents had been killed, he instantly got angry. It was the first time she thought she might have to restrain her brother. But he was always in control, pulling back just before he lost it. She should have expected that, she realized.

When she finished telling him everything, his chest was rising and falling rapidly like he was hyperventilating. She could see the emotion pouring out of him. That was how she had felt when she learned Adler had murdered their parents. Telling Clark about it had sparked her anger all over again. She wanted to charge after the albino right then, and she tried, but it was Clark who stopped her. His passion had reignited her fire, and he had stopped her from doing what she had wanted to from the beginning.

"No," Clark said, holding onto her before she left the place she now shared with Sophia. "We don't take him out yet. We don't do anything yet. We plan his demise. Just wait, and one day he'll suffer. I promise."

Her brother's words played in her head, reminding her of the revenge she craved. But she also had to be the voice of reason for Clark. They did that for each other.

"Yes, I'm sure," Liv said adamantly, her eyes flicking to the Black Void on the other side of Clark. She didn't trust speaking right there, or really anywhere in the House of Seven. Even though Adler and Decar were gone, she still couldn't shake the feeling that someone else was in the House, watching them. Sneaking. Doing something. But Liv also reasoned that it could be paranoia. It was an easy thing to fall victim to after learning that your parents were murdered by someone who was supposed to be on their side.

"Are you sure the chamber is empty?" Liv asked in a whisper.

Clark nodded. "Except for the regulators. They are always in there."

Liv didn't think Jude and Diabolos would be an issue. Their job was to call out when someone was deceitful during the meetings. The magical animals were just like the lophos she'd encountered at the monastery. They didn't need food to survive, and they didn't age. Their job was timeless and required them to always be present and accountable to the council.

"Okay, I'll go first," Liv said, stepping through the Door of Reflection. She expected to see something ridiculous in the vision of her latest fear, like her wearing the awful dress Rudolf had picked out for the wedding. However, the image that burned across her vision wasn't as trivial as that previous fear.

In the vision, Liv stood on the top of a hill, looking down at a battlefield. A great war raged below her as magicians and mortals slaughtered each other. The mortals had guns and tanks, and the magicians fought with swords and blasts of fire. Neither side appeared to be winning, but rather, each alienated the other.

"What if I'm wrong?" Liv heard herself say out loud. The thought brought a gasp to her mouth. She hadn't hesitated to unearth the truth, to pick up the mission her parents had started, but she'd never stopped to wonder if she should. Adler was a bad man; that was obvious. But what if he or whoever had started this was right? What if mortals *weren't* supposed to be in the House? What if allowing them to see magic again would ruin everything?

There was no history book she could turn to in order to find out exactly what had gone wrong. All of that had been covered up. And so, the question plagued her mind.

What if revealing the truth was wrong? What if another war would come out of it?

Everything would be her fault.

Liv shook off the image of fires raging and death on the battlefield as she stepped all the way through the Door of Reflection.

It was strange to stand in the middle of the Chamber of the Tree without the council peering down at her or any other Warriors in the space. Overhead, the twinkling lights of the Tree shone down on Liv, reminding her of the mission they'd come here for: to unregister their magic.

She'd been in the chamber many times lately and had forgotten to study the Tree behind the council's bench. The names of the Seven were depicted on its massive branches. How different would it look when they revealed the truth?

Clark entered the chamber a moment later, appearing disoriented, as most did after passing through the Door of Reflection.

"Did you have a vision of you wearing a t-shirt?" Liv asked him.

"Ha-ha," he said, not appearing amused. "My worst nightmares aren't of me wearing relaxed clothing."

"Oh, are your nightmares of a world where there's no hair gel? The inhumanity of it all!"

Clark shook his head, setting up a privacy spell in the chamber. "I have real fears, you know. Ones that involve you and Sophia."

Liv nodded, not liking that he had gotten real. It would

have been better for her if they merely made fun of each other during the time they were in there.

"So, do you think you can unregister us?" Liv asked.

"Well, I shouldn't be able to without the other Councilors," he stated, striding over the bench. "However, if Adler was able to lock our family's magic without anyone else, then it has to be possible."

Liv was about to pull out her phone to call Alicia, who she trusted to help and who would know how to work around the magical tech. However, right then, the white tiger sauntered around the side of the bench. She almost didn't pay him any notice, thinking he was simply there to chill and observe, as usual.

There was something different about Jude this time, though, Liv realized. His body weight slid backward on his hind legs, and his green eyes narrowed. If Liv wasn't mistaken, he appeared ready to attack.

Clark, who was focused on getting to the bench, hadn't seen the white tiger. He hurried forward, crossing Jude's path just as Liv realized what was going to happen next.

"Watch out!" she yelled, throwing her hand into the air. A blast of wind shot from it, hitting Jude straight in the chest as he reared back on his hind legs, his massive paws stretched out on either side of him like he was about to bear-hug Clark.

He shot back, knocking into the far wall from the force.

The floor under their feet shook, and the lights flickered. A cold blast of wind streamed into the chamber from somewhere, making the temperature drop instantly.

"What have you done?" Clark yelled, glaring between the white tiger crumpled beside the wall and Liv.

"I had to!" she said, pulling out Bellator. "He was going to attack you."

"That's because I'm doing something wrong, Liv."

She shook her head, striding cautiously over. "The privacy spell will protect others from finding out about this. We've got to hurry."

"But what if you've killed him," Clark argued. "How are we going to explain that?"

"I didn't kill him," she stated. "I just protected you. You're welcome."

If she were honest with herself, Jude did appear to be dead, his head resting to the side by his paws and the rest of his body looked lifeless.

What if she had killed one of the regulators for the House? How would they explain it? She'd taken out the good regulator. What did that make her?

Clark had done what she'd suggested, hurrying to his spot on the bench and getting to work. He was scrolling through his codex.

Liv halted when she reached the top of the bench. It was strange to peer down on the chamber floor from there, judging those who stood on the Warrior's places. How different the Councilors' positions were. They had comfortable seats up high, while the Warriors stood on the ground, looking up at them. Behind them was a narrow platform where books and other supplies apparently used to be stored for reference. That was before they had moved to digital codices and magic tech. Presently that space was empty.

"I really don't understand how I'm supposed to do this,"

Clark grumbled, scrolling through his codex. "It shouldn't work for only one Councilor."

Liv dialed Alicia, relieved when she picked up after only one ring.

"Hey, birdie," she said to the Italian when she answered.

Alicia didn't think this nickname was funny, but she laughed anyway.

"Remember when you offered to help if I ever needed something done with complicated magical tech?" Liv asked over the phone.

"Of course," Alicia answered.

"Well, I'm calling in the favor," she said, handing the phone to Clark, who looked at her reluctantly.

It wasn't advisable to loop anyone else into what they were doing. However, without Alicia, they wouldn't unregister their magic, so they'd fall victim to Adler's attacks the same way their family did.

After shooting Liv a frustrated expression, Clark took the phone.

"She can help," Liv said encouragingly.

Clark nodded, sticking the phone to his ear.

Feeling proud, Liv lifted her chin and surveyed the room. That was when she saw it. Or rather, lack of it.

Jude was gone.

## CHAPTER NINETEEN

"What is it?" Clark said, pulling the phone away from his face as he took in Liv's panicked expression.

She shook her head, scanning the chamber. "It's nothing. Just explain the situation to Alicia. We need her expertise."

Clark didn't appear to believe Liv as he slowly raised the phone back to his face.

Was it really a problem that Jude had disappeared after trying to attack Clark? Liv tried to tell herself it wasn't a big deal. When that didn't work, she told herself she'd mistaken the whole thing. The white tiger would never attack. He'd only ever been stoic and graceful when she'd been in the Chamber of the Tree.

And yet, every second she couldn't find him filled her with dread. Liv edged down the stairs from the high bench, constantly scanning the area for a sign of the regulator.

"It's a complicated bit of magic tech," Clark said in an

impatient voice. "I don't think turning it off and back on is going to help."

"Just do whatever she says," Liv ordered, her focus on the many dark spots in the circular room.

Her brother shot her an angry expression. "But she wants me to turn off the entire system. I shouldn't be able to do that."

"And one Councilor shouldn't be able to unregister us or lock our magic on their own, and yet we know that they can," Liv stated.

Alicia's voice came through the phone, her irritation evident from her high-pitched tone. Clark pulled the phone away from his ear, his eyes widening.

"You helped create this system?" he said in disbelief.

"That makes sense," Liv said dryly, putting her back to the wall as she sidestepped, continuing to look for the white tiger. There shouldn't have been places for him to hide, since he was huge at over four hundred pounds. However, that was one of the many mysteries of the Chamber of the Tree. The dark pockets around the room were like separate places where the regulator often disappeared. Conversely, Diabolos often hung out up high, where the ceiling met the walls.

"If I reboot the system, will anyone be able to tell?" Clark asked Alicia over the phone.

A moment later, he let out a deep breath. "Okay, fine. I'm ready to do it. How long will it take?"

He glanced at Liv. "She says two minutes. Then we'll have a small window where the security settings aren't up, and we can unregister our magic."

"How do we keep the council from finding out I'm not

registered anymore?" Liv asked, knowing they were constantly monitoring her magic use for various reasons. That was common for Warriors, to ensure they weren't abusing their powers or to check that they were safe in the field.

Clark listened to the scientist over the phone and then nodded. "All you need to do is stand on your place while I'm unregistering you. Alicia says there's a way to loop your magic feed from the last several months so it looks like the present reports."

Liv liked this idea. It was similar to when criminals in movies looped the security cameras so the unsuspecting guards didn't realize they'd been tricked.

"Okay, let's get this going," Liv said, striding toward her spot on the far side of the chamber. She took her place and gave Clark a hopeful smile. "Two minutes and we'll be done."

He let out a strained breath, patches of red covering his face the same way they always did when he was nervous. "Okay, ready in three, two, one."

One by one, the lights representing registered magicians blinked off overhead. The lit-up branches of the tree dimmed, receding toward the base of the trunk until they were in complete darkness. Liv blinked, feeling suddenly blind. Then she caught a movement of light on the bench from the phone pressed to Clark's face—and behind him, she saw the glowing green eyes of the white tiger, perched on the broad shelf in back of the bench.

CHAPTER TWENTY

Liv didn't even think. She just reacted, summoning a fireball and launching it. A scream ripped out of Clark's mouth as he dove for the floor behind the bench. Jude soared overhead, the fireball missing him by inches and crashing into the wall behind him.

The white tiger landed in front of Liv, his long sharp teeth bared as a growl spilled out of his mouth, echoing all over the room.

Liv already had another fireball ready, both for protection and for light. Jude began to sidestep, his pensive stare on Liv.

"What's gotten into you?" Liv asked him, wondering if he could respond somehow. "We're not doing anything wrong."

The white tiger's growl shook Liv at her core, like she was standing next to a loudspeaker at a rock concert.

"Okay, it may seem wrong to unregister our magic, but it's to keep us safe," Liv explained. "And where have you been when Adler has been locking magicians' magic and whatever else?"

Liv thought she'd brought up an excellent point, but the white tiger's expression was unchanging.

Clark stood up again, his eyes wide with fright, the cell phone pressed to his face as he whispered to Alicia.

"I don't want to hurt you," Liv stated to Jude. "Just let us do what we need to do, and then we'll be out of here."

The white tiger lunged for Liv, making her dive forward, rolling over one shoulder. She threw the fireball to the side of him, knowing it wouldn't hit him, but hoping it would keep him back as she reloaded.

"Seriously?" Liv yelled. "This isn't even a meeting of the Seven. Don't you take a day off?"

Jude's large paw came up, swiping through the air. His reach was longer than Liv realized, making her release the fireball to keep him from mauling her face. The tiger growled as he cowered back, his eyes on fire with rage.

Liv summoned two more fireballs, swiftly moving her hands back and forth to discourage him from jumping at her again. "And Seven, really?" she continued. "You know damn well it's the House of Fourteen. You have to. But you're not jumping all over the Councilors when they casually refer to the Seven, are you?"

This seemed to strike a chord with the white tiger. Or maybe it was the hypnotizing effects of the fireballs as she moved them through the air, the light from them blurring slightly.

"His job is to stop any treachery," Clark said from the bench. "You can't reason with him. He supports truths and tries to banish deceit."

"But we're deceiving so we can stay alive!" Liv yelled furiously as the tiger made another attempt to attack her. She dropped both of her fireballs, and they extinguished on the floor immediately. Before she could summon another one, Jude's claws were in her back as his weight crushed her to the floor. She tried to scream, but her breath was knocked out of her when the beast crashed into her.

"Liv!" Clark yelled from high up.

The pain that spread across Liv's back as the white tiger clawed her was excruciating. It felt like more than just claws and teeth. It was like she was being shoved through a meat grinder. They rolled twice, Jude's weight adding insult to injury each time he was on top of her.

In the pure darkness of the chamber, Liv couldn't see anything, not that light would help at this point. She was imprisoned in the unrelenting grasp of this regulator.

"I need to turn the system back on!" Clark yelled into the phone. "I need to do something!"

He was stuck up high, trying to work with Alicia. There was no way for him to save Liv. Lights would have helped with that, but in the pitch-black, he was helpless, and that made her feel remorseful for him. Her pity didn't last for long, because in a swift movement, Jude was off of her.

She didn't understand why he'd backed off, but she managed to push herself back several feet, cradling her arms around her knees. Her reserves were low from the attack, but if she could calm herself enough, she could summon another fireball. Maybe pull Bellator. Do anything to help protect her from the regulator, whose present location was unclear.

Then she felt his hot breath and knew his attacks weren't over. The snarl that came next sent a sharp chill down Liv's injured back. She didn't know whether to dive to the right or left or how to escape what would come next.

The lights flickered on and back off, illuminating the white tiger. He was right in front of Liv, his face inches from hers. She shuffled backward, trying to get to her feet, but unable to get up due to the lacerations on her back. Like a strobe light, she got strange glimpses of Jude's progress after her as the lights kicked on and then back off again and again.

His white face looked wrong, covered in her blood. She used all her energy to push to her feet, pulling Bellator at the same moment. What she did next would be impossible to cover up. The Council would know they'd been there. There would be no way to hide that she killed the ancient beast.

What happened next was completely in slow motion. Bringing Bellator up and around, Liv threw all her strength into the movement. Simultaneously, the tiger growled, swinging his giant paw through the air at her. Either the sword or his paw would connect first, but one of them wasn't going to be standing in a few seconds.

And then the sound of the crow overhead froze them both. Bellator stopped inches from Jude's face. Similarly, his paw halted in midair only a breath away from Liv. Diabolos dove at the two of them. Afraid of another attack, Liv threw herself backward, bringing Bellator behind her as she kept her weight low.

An explosion of smoke and ash rained down on them as a strange flapping noise filled the air. It seemed to come from everywhere and nowhere at the same time. It rang in Liv's head, making her think she was imagining it, but then it shook the floor under her feet. Liv knew Jude heard it too, for his head fell to the stone under him as he covered his ears with his paws.

Her teeth vibrated from the noise, which grew in intensity second by second. She tried to shake off the strangeness, but suddenly she felt drugged. Ash continued to fall from up high, covering her feet and making it hard to move. Clark was yelling at her from the bench.

She couldn't hear him. The flapping drowned everything.

He was waving his arms wildly in the air, then he pointed to the middle of the room. Liv couldn't understand what he was trying to say, and then she saw it. Nearly covered by the ash, but still glowing: her spot in the chamber!

Jude looked up when she sprinted for her place. Each step was harder than the last. The distance seemed impossibly far. Liv recognized the fire in the tiger's eyes as he threw himself to his feet. This wasn't over yet.

He was about to lunge at her. She was only a few feet from the glowing circle marking her spot. If she didn't get there in time, they would fail. She would die, slain by an animal meant to protect the truth.

The irony wasn't lost on her.

An explosion threw Liv off balance, and the chamber shook. She covered her head, unsure of what was happening. Scorching flames seemed to lick at her from everywhere, making her cringe into a ball as she covered her head. There were two loud bangs. The walls shook. A growl was followed by a loud caw.

Suddenly the air was frigid. Nervous about what she'd see when she unfolded her arms from over her head, Liv tentatively peered around when the floor was no longer shaking and pushed up to a crouch. Jude lay lifeless a few feet from her. She let out a gasp, the urge to check his vitals pulsing through her.

*Was he dead?* she wondered just as a small ticking sound drew her attention to something on the other side of her.

Diabolos, similar to Jude, laid on the floor on the other side of her. Although he was moving slightly, they were pained movements.

Liv suddenly felt dizzy, and there was a strange copper taste in her mouth. Then she remembered that she needed to get to her spot before it was too late, but as she looked around, she realized that somehow she was already there.

Drips echoed around the room. Liv looked up, thinking there must have been a leak in the ceiling, but there wasn't. She glanced down, disorientation about to overwhelm her, and realized where the dripping was coming from. It was her blood, hitting the chamber floor in fat drops.

That was the last thing she saw before her legs gave out. Her head hit the floor beside Diabolos, and her feet splayed across Jude.

## CHAPTER TWENTY-ONE

*S*he was going to die, and it would all be his fault, Clark thought, rushing through the House of Seven, checking every corridor.

After whatever that was that had happened in the Chamber of the Tree, Clark had rushed over to Liv. She was breathing, but her wounds were bad. He could tell that much. And then there were Jude and Diabolos. They were barely alive.

He wasn't sure exactly what had happened, even though he had watched it all from the bench. The crow seemed to have exploded, sending ash all over the chamber. Then, when Liv had dashed for the lit spot on the ground, Jude had gone after her. Diabolos had crashed into him, just over Liv's head, and both had fallen to the floor, unconscious. It was the strangest thing he'd ever seen, and that was saying a lot.

In the sitting room, he finally found Hester, having her afternoon tea. The old healer appeared so civilized, reading a book and chewing on a biscuit.

"Hester," he began, realizing he was close to hyperventilating. "I need your help. It's a matter of urgency."

She glanced up casually and without hesitation rose to her feet. "Well, let's go, then."

"O-o-ohhhh…" he said, having thought he would have to convince her. "It's Liv. She's in the—"

Hester shook her head at him, sharpness in her gray eyes. "I know where she is, but no one else needs to," she said, glancing around at the walls like they had ears.

"You do?" he asked, surprised.

"Of course, dear. Everything that happens next has been predicted."

Clark thought he was going to throw up. "Then, will others know about this?"

"Unless they are Trudy, who had the prediction, I suspect not," Hester told him, hurrying out of the room.

So Trudy was a seer. That made sense. The DeVries were an old magical family, most of them having unique abilities like Hester, who could heal. And Clark knew why they hadn't advertised that Trudy could see the future. Things had had a way of happening to magicians like that over the centuries.

Clark sped after the old magician, surprised by how fast she moved. "What happened in the prediction? Will she be okay?"

Hester stopped when the hallway split and shook her head. "No, she dies."

Bile flooded into Clark's mouth. He tried to say something, but Hester had already hurried off.

When he finally caught up with her, he choked on his words. Hester was being extra cautious as she moved through the House, stopping at every bend to check that they weren't being followed.

Catching the expression on his face, she shook her head, leaning close. She whispered, "You left her, and I know why. But in the vision Trudy saw, Jude wasn't dead, and he wasn't done with her."

*What?*

That one word echoed for a long time in Clark's head. He'd left Liv to die. It was unfathomable. He would never live with himself.

"B-b-but..."

Hester didn't give him a chance to say anything, just continued down the corridor.

Clark shook off the fear and dread and picked up his speed, racing in the direction of the chamber, leaving Hester behind. Everything blurred as he shot through the House, racing toward his sister. He didn't have his father's cane, but he'd fight Jude with his bare hands if he needed to. Whatever it took to save his sister. Guilt was a bomb in his head, ready to detonate. It was going to explode once he entered the Chamber of the Tree and saw what he'd done.

Quickly he passed through the Door of Reflection, pushing the visions of failing his family out of his mind. It wasn't just a sick potential anymore. It was becoming a reality.

Clark halted when he stumbled through the door. Liv wasn't dead, but she wasn't safe either.

Trudy DeVries stood between Jude and Liv, who was still passed out on the floor. The Warrior held a sword on the white tiger, who was snarling, his head swinging to the side in an act of aggression. She didn't waiver from her place, protecting his sister.

When Jude caught sight of Clark, the tiger rounded on him, his stance indicating he was ready to pounce. In a matter of seconds, the strongest animal Clark had ever faced was about to soar through the air and attack. He wasn't as fast as Liv. He wasn't brave. But he had one thing she didn't.

Clark Beaufont dropped to one knee, bowing his head in humility. "Jude, regulator for the House, we broke the rules. We unregistered our magic. We did it because our family was deceived. My parents' magic was locked when they were on the Matterhorn, and they were overpowered by Adler Sinclair. We did what we had to do, not because we are trying to deceive the House, but because we are trying to protect it. We cannot do it if we are dead."

Clark's words ran out too fast. He had nothing else to say to prove his point. He felt the white tiger's gaze heavy on him. When he looked up, he was stunned to find that the regulator's stance was suddenly different. He wasn't poised to attack, but rather sitting on his hind legs, his tail swishing back and forth and a calm expression on his face, like how he usually appeared during meetings.

For several seconds, Clark was speechless. Then Hester's hand clamped down on his shoulder, and he nearly jumped clear up to the ceiling.

"Only words that were one-hundred-percent honest could have quelled Jude," the healer said. "Well done, Councilor Beaufont."

Clark rose, shaking his head. "But Liv tried to explain the same thing to him before he attacked her."

"But you two were also in the midst of doing something he deemed wrong," Hester explained. "He can't hear the truth and see wrong being done and understand it. That is too confusing for Jude."

The healer hurried off, but not to Liv, as Clark expected. She scooped up Diabolos, cradling the limp crow in her arms.

"What about Liv?" Clark asked, hurrying over.

Hester glanced over her shoulder. "She'll be fine once she sleeps it off. Jude's attacks are purely mental."

"But I saw her bleeding," Clark said, revolving to find the blood that had splattered the floor. It was nowhere in sight. The ash that had littered the floor was gone too. He did a full circle before facing Hester and Trudy with a questioning look.

"It's a very real experience when a regulator defends their pillar," Trudy explained as Hester went to work on Diabolos. "It is real for the person who is being attacked and the one watching. I'm sure it was awful to watch your sister go through something like that."

Clark nodded, but then shook his head. "I didn't see much of it, actually. We were in the dark. But I heard her screams, and I felt that there was nothing I could do to save her."

"Did you do what you two came here for?" Trudy asked.

"Unregister our magic?" Clark asked. "Yes, but I need to explain what—"

Trudy cut him off with a shake of her head. "There's no reason to explain to me. I know why you two were here. I'm grateful I pieced together that today was when it would happen, or I might not have shown up in time to save her."

"But you said Jude's attacks were purely mental?" Clark asked.

"Yes, but what happens to the mind can influence the body," Trudy explained.

Clark had many questions running through his mind but was cut off by the flapping of wings as Diabolos awoke in Hester's arms. The crow took off at once, flying over to where Jude now sat next to the bench. He landed next to the white tiger and glanced up at him with a strange expression in his eyes, as if he were grateful to be beside a longtime friend again.

Hester let out a sigh of relief. "Well, that will deplete me for the better part of the week. I haven't had to bring back anything so powerful in…well, I do believe this was a first."

Trudy offered her sister her arm. "Please let me take you up to your room."

Hester shook her off. "I'm fine for now. I have many questions for you, though, Councilor Beaufont."

Clark gulped. There would be so many questions. He wished Liv were awake to help him answer them. To explain. But she was still peacefully asleep on the floor of the chamber.

"You were able to unregister your magic by yourself?" Hester asked.

"Well, yes. But we had to—"

"After hearing what happened to your family, I absolutely agree," Hester stated.

"And we would have come to the council with this information, but—"

The healer shook her head. "I think we all know that it's unsafe and unwise to voice our concerns about such things openly. You were right to keep this a secret."

"Liv and I plan to—"

In unison, both sisters adamantly shook their heads. "Please don't tell us your plans. It's better that we don't know in case anything happens," Hester said.

"You're not going to say anything to the council about this?" Clark asked, having trouble computing what was happening here. He knew Hester and Trudy were on their side, but it was also hard to trust anyone after all he'd learned.

Trudy gave her sister a questioning look. "Say anything about what?"

Hester shrugged. "I'm not sure. Do you think the chef is serving cucumber soup with dinner tonight?"

Trudy thought for a moment. "I'm not sure, but I hope so. I could use something refreshing."

Hester rubbed her hands together as if she were trying to warm herself. "Oh, me too. Although if I were sleeping on the chamber floor right now, soup wouldn't be what I needed when I awoke."

The sisters strode for the exit together. "Oh, really? What would you have, then?" Trudy asked in a loud voice.

"I'm thinking cake. Maybe ice cream cake. Possible both ice cream and cake," Hester replied.

When they were at the Door of Reflection, Hester

turned back to a bewildered Clark. "I do wish we could help you more, Councilor, but something tells me that the Beaufonts are the only ones who can save us from what happens next."

Trudy elbowed her sister in the side. "I prefer not to be called 'something.'"

Hester nodded. "I know you do. My apologies." She disappeared through the Door of Reflection a moment later.

Trudy glanced thoughtfully at Liv before offering Clark a sympathetic expression. "I've seen the future play out many different ways recently. It always turns to black if anyone but a Beaufont intervenes. I hope you know we'd help if we thought it would make a difference."

The warrior disappeared through the Door of Reflection, and Clark knew she was right. His ancestors had ensured that the Beaufonts didn't forget the truth. That was their role in all this, whether one thought of it as a blessing or a curse, and therefore, no one but a Beaufont could finish this.

He and Liv might die trying to do what came next, but they were going to do it together.

This ended with them.

## CHAPTER TWENTY-TWO

Liv was seconds away from chucking Clark across the room.

"Didn't Hester say I should have cake and ice cream?" she asked, shoving the chicken noodle soup away.

"Yes," he said, wiping his hands on the apron tied around his waist. "But we have to think about nutrition as well as magical reserves. One might go up, but the other one down if you're not careful."

Liv grimaced at the floor. "Why is it that everyone keeps lecturing about my diet lately?"

"Maybe it's because we're worried about your choices," Clark said, indicating the still-full glass of water on the tray over her lap.

"Yes, I plan on drinking that. As soon as you give me something proper it can wash down," Liv stated, sitting up taller in her bed. That was where she'd found herself that morning. She'd expected to find long claw marks down her back, but there hadn't been any. Then Clark had appeared with an inadequate tray of food and an explanation that involved Hester and Trudy, who was apparently a seer.

"Fine," Clark stated. "What do you want to eat?"

"Ice cream," Liv said definitively.

"Liv, it's morning," he argued as Sophia showed up, peeking around the doorframe.

"Yes, ice cream for breakfast is a fantastic idea," Liv said. "Make it two bowls, one for me and one for Sophia. Unless you want to join us. We're eating them in bed. Maybe with our shoes on in bed. Oh, and I'm not going to wash my hands either."

Clark rolled his eyes and stomped out of the room.

Sophia slipped around the doorframe, covering her grin until Clark was gone. Then she allowed the giggle to spill from her mouth. "He'd be so mad at you right now if you weren't laid up in bed."

Liv shook her head. "You're welcome. You get to benefit from my predicament. Have you ever had ice cream for breakfast?"

"No, usually Clark makes me eat oatmeal without any sugar and a green smoothie that tastes like dirty feet."

Grimacing, Liv said, "Well, not today. Or tomorrow, even. Life is too short to eat things that make us want to gag."

"He says that I'll live longer if I eat those things, though."

"Sure, you'll live longer, but what's the point?" Liv reasoned. She patted the spot next to her in the bed. "Come on. Let's cuddle up, and you can tell me what you've been up to while I've been on boring adventures."

Sophia smiled. "I know you've been doing crazy, death-defying stuff."

"I faced a magical tiger who did crazy stuff to my head but apparently nothing to my body," Liv corrected. "What about you and Morgan? What's new with you two?"

Sophia took the spot next to Liv in the bed, seeming to relish in the opportunity to cuddle. "His name isn't Morgan."

"Oh, really?" Liv asked. "I thought you were going with a traditional name for the dragon? Simon, maybe? Donald, possibly? Or even George?"

Sophia pulled the covers over her head when Clark reentered, carrying a tray with two bowls of ice cream, a reluctant expression on his face. "You know, although you're recovering from magical depletion, Soph isn't."

Liv took the bowl he offered her and passed it to her little sister. "No, she's only a child, and you know how many times you get back the chance to be young again? Oh, wait."

He shook his head, a disapproving expression on his face. "I'm only trying to look out for—"

"Our best interests," Liv said, cutting him off as she took the other bowl on the tray. "I totally appreciate that. But would you mind going to get me another serving of ice cream?"

His brow furrowed. "You haven't finished that one yet."

"I know, but I will, and then I'll be hungry." Liv gave Sophia a questioning expression. "How am I when I get hungry?"

Sophia stuck a large spoonful of chocolate ice cream into her mouth. "You don't want to know. It's awful."

"Liv…" Clark said, a warning in his voice.

"It's like I turn into a white tiger and maul people, although I get that you wouldn't know what that's like since you were protected by someone in the chamber," Liv said casually.

"Oh, fine," Clark said, defeat heavy in his tone as he stomped for the exit.

Sophia and Liv giggled as they shoveled more ice cream into their mouths. It did make her feel better, but what was actually healing her was being there with her sister and brother. She and Clark had done what they set out to do. Their magic was unregistered. Their tracks were covered. And they were that much closer to stopping Adler Sinclair. She just had to find him.

The anywhere pad Rory had given her lay beside her bed. It lit up suddenly, gaining both girls' attention. Sliding her bowl onto her lap, Liv pulled the pad to her. Rory had sent her a message.

*We have the* Forgotten Archives.

"*Forgotten Archives?*" Sophia asked, peering over Liv's shoulder. She swore the little girl was getting bigger every single day. Soon she'd be taller than her, which wouldn't take much.

"Yeah, same question here." Liv pulled her pen from the bedside table.

*What are the* Forgotten Archives?

*That's the lost history. Activating the book will make it so mortals and magical creatures remember the correct history.*

*Cool,* Liv wrote. *Activate it.*

*We can't,* Rory replied. *Not until mortals can see magic again.*

"Of course," Liv said with a growl.

"Ask him if he's okay," Sophia said.

"Well, he's writing me notes, so I think that it implies he's okay, or at least not dead," Liv replied.

"Still ask him," Sophia encouraged.

Liv nodded and wrote: *How are you and Mum?*

A minute later, a message appeared.

*Tell Sophia we're fine and thanks for asking, although Mum says you should call her Mrs. Laurens.*

Liv laughed. "Can't fool that woman, can I?" She pulled the anywhere pad closer.

*Is Decar still after you? Do you need help?*

Rory answered after a short pause.

*Yes, he's after us, but we don't need your help.*

*Are you sure? I'm not doing anything right now.*

Sophia giggled, taking a large spoonful of melting ice cream.

*Sometimes we rely on you too much, Liv,* Rory's reply said. *You've gotten us this far. This mission is one we must complete on our own, for you.*

"Oh, that's so sweet," Sophia gushed.

Liv thought for a moment.

*Is that what Mrs. Laurens told you to say to keep me away? She doesn't want me there annoying her, does she?*

*And here I thought I was being diplomatic,* Rory replied.

*Okay, well, be safe, and knock Decar out,* Liv wrote, not wanting to go into the full story on a magical pad of paper. She'd have to tell Rory in person what she'd learned about the Sinclairs. Still, it was impossible not to worry about him and Bermuda.

*We will. I'll see you soon,* Rory stated.

*Sounds good. Don't die,* she replied as Clark re-entered the room, holding a tray with a single bowl of ice cream.

"You haven't even eaten the first bowl I got for you," Clark whined. "This one is going to be melted by the time you get to it."

Liv nodded, scooting over in the bed. "Then it seems like you better get in here and eat it for me."

Clark gave her an indignant expression that said, "You can't be serious."

She patted the place beside her. "Come on. When was the last time you had anything fun for breakfast that wasn't loaded with fiber and tasted like cardboard?"

"Liv…" he said, seeming to try to restrain his patience.

"Clark…" she replied, matching his tone. "You only live once. Will you please indulge your sisters and curl up and eat breakfast in bed? We really don't ask for a lot."

He glanced down at his attire. "But I'm wearing—"

"Incredibly starched clothes," Liv interrupted. "They will survive lounging in a bed for a half-hour."

"A half-hour?" he asked incredulously.

"Oh, yes, Clark Beaufont," Liv said, taking the tray from his hands. "You're going to lounge and eat ice cream for at least a half-hour. If I had a television, we'd also be watching cartoons."

"Why do you not have a television?" Sophia asked.

"Firstly, I'm too busy to watch anything," Liv said, pulling Clark down next to her. Thankfully he allowed it, although he kept his shoes to the side, off the mattress. "And also, I've been looking for the perfect time to get one."

Liv wrinkled her nose, trying to think of exactly what she wanted. A moment later, she pointed at the wall across from her bed. The perfect-sized flat screen television appeared on the wall, hung at the right height.

"I'm guessing this was the perfect time, then?" Clark asked, sitting rigidly next to her.

She handed him the bowl of ice cream and nodded. "Yes, and if you don't eat this, it will melt, and you'll be on the naughty list for the rest of your life."

"Liv…"

"Clark, we have so much left to do. We have bad guys to defeat and wounds to heal and people to save. If what Trudy said is true, then it's us who has to fix this. So for right now, let the Beaufonts just enjoy some rare time together where we can pretend we're just kids."

"Hey!" Sophia grunted, drawing attention to her.

"Or just *be* kids," Liv corrected.

Clark actually smiled, picking up his spoon dripping with ice cream. "Yeah, I guess you're right. To the Beaufonts."

Liv and Sophia clanked their spoons against his before they all took a bite, snuggling together as they'd never been able to do before.

Because even heroes needed a day off. That way, they could rise up and stomp out an evil that had been allowed to exist for entirely too long.

## CHAPTER TWENTY-THREE

The loneliness was close to biting Adler Sinclair in half. Being by himself in the facility on the Matterhorn was taking its toll.

He missed having Indikos being beside him. It wasn't that the two got along exceptionally well or understood each other. He'd actually struggled for years to understand what the miniature dragon needed. However, he liked to know that Indikos was there. It made him feel protected.

Currently, the howling wind reminded Adler that he was on the top of this dangerous mountain by himself. The electricity flickered regularly, making his job even more difficult.

He didn't need the electricity to power the signal. It was fueled by magic tech. And he didn't need electricity for the upgrade he was doing, but he needed light to focus.

"This is the worst place in the world," Adler fired, throwing the tool in his hand across the room. He couldn't think of a more awful place to be, but soon, he could leave the revolting place. Olivia Beaufont wouldn't be able to stay away; he was sure of it. She'd come after him, and when she did, he'd be ready. Then he could finish her off and be done with the Beaufonts once and for all. It was all coming to an end, and not at all too soon.

Adler was tired of this ongoing battle. Talon should have had a more decisive win when he defeated the mortals. He should have. If he had done it the way Adler would have, this wouldn't have been a problem.

The God Magician had always thought Father Time was the biggest obstacle to his success, keeping him from rising to full power and living without restriction for eternity. However, he was wrong. It had been mortals, and Adler knew it.

Soon they would no longer be a problem.

He pulled away from the giant piece of magic tech that Talon had invented centuries ago. It was incredible, broadcasting a signal that kept mortals from seeing magic. And soon it would do so much more.

Using his finger and things he'd learned from his great-great-grandfather, Adler fused wires together using his magic. When the job was complete, he sat back, wondering if he'd done what he thought he had.

Taking a deep breath, he put in the code that would implement the changes he'd made. It was impossible for him to know from where he sat if it had worked. For that, he'd need eyes on the ground.

He pulled his phone from his pocket, knowing the signal would work even though he was in the middle of nowhere, or, as Talon had called it, the beginning of the end. The Matterhorn was the place the God Magician had deduced was the best to disrupt the magical source of energy connected to mortals.

And what better place from which to end them all?

The phone rang three times before the person on the other end picked up.

"I've activated the signal with the upgrades," Adler said.

"What would you have me do, Master?" the woman on the other side of the line asked.

He huffed with frustration. "What do you think? Keep an eye on mortals worldwide. Note and document any widespread changes."

"Changes, sir?" she asked.

"Epidemics," he stated.

## CHAPTER TWENTY-FOUR

"Rudolf just had to go off and get married," Liv said, hopping around on one foot, trying to find her other high heel. It was difficult to see the floor with the long dress dragging all over it.

"I don't think you mind him getting married as much as that he made you his best man," Sophia said, sitting on the edge of Liv's bed and kicking her feet back and forth as she watched her dig under the dresser for the missing shoe.

"Yes, that's exactly the part I mind." Liv grunted, reaching blindly under the dresser and feeling around. "I'm not meant to go to these kinds of events and wear uncomfortable clothes and make small talk with annoying fae."

"Be careful, or you're going to mess up your hair," Sophia cautioned.

"Then I just won't be able to go," Liv said with a shrug.

"You have to go," Sophia squealed. "You look like a movie star."

Victorious, Liv pulled her other high heel out from under the dresser. She slipped it on and took her spot in front of the full-length mirror. Sophia was right. Liv didn't look at all like herself. She did in fact appear like she was about to walk down the red carpet at some fancy event in her tight-fitting ball gown with its long train. The greens and pinks changed depending on the light or the room or some other factor Liv couldn't figure out, and the flowers had stopped blooming long enough for her to get ready, which was good because they made it even harder to move around.

Rudolf had informed Liv that the flowers would bloom when she felt love. The idea was that during the ceremony, after Rudolf and Serena exchanged vows, the wedding party's attire would all bloom as the couple exchanged their first kiss as husband and wife.

Liv had to refrain from barfing after learning this. Still, she had to admit that Rudolf's romantic side had come out in preparation for the big affair.

Sophia had helped with her hair and makeup, arranging her long strands into the shapes of flowers and inter-twining pearls in her soft curls. Her makeup was soft and natural, highlighting her features without making her look like a whore.

"I think you're missing something," Sophia said, tilting her head to the side and regarding Liv with a tentative expression.

"The list is long, actually," Liv grumbled. "Boots, for starters. Undergarments would be nice as well—"

"Rudolf said they'd disrupt the look of the dress," Sophia cut in.

"Yes, and since when did I allow Rudolf Sweetwater to tell me whether I can or can't wear a bra?" Liv said, fisting her hands on her hips. "I mean, I get that men are usually insisting we wear that uncomfortable garment, but he really shouldn't have a say in what I put on my body."

"He just wants you to look as radiant as possible," Sophia argued. "And you will. Especially because I have something for you."

Liv dropped her chin and gave her sister a look of surprise when a small flat box appeared in her small hands. "Please tell me my cape is in that box."

Sophia giggled. "No, but it's something of our mother's."

The smile on Liv's face disappeared. "Soph…you didn't."

Her sister nodded. "I did. And it's perfect for this occasion."

Guinevere Beaufont was very similar to her daughter, not caring for jewelry or other fashion-related items. However, her mother had owned one necklace that stuck out in Liv's memory. First, she only wore it on the most special occasions. Secondly, it was the most beautiful piece of jewelry Liv had ever seen.

"You went to the House and got it?" Liv asked, realizing that her hands were shaking.

She couldn't imagine wearing her mother's necklace. It was like she'd graduated to some new realm where child-hood dreams were possible. How many times had she imagined herself dancing and wearing her mother's finest piece of jewelry?

For a child who hadn't played dress-up, it was the only time that Liv remembered wanting to be a princess, but that was mostly because of the way her mother had looked on the few occasions she'd seen her wearing it. Guinevere didn't look like a princess in the heavy emerald and diamond encrusted necklace. She'd looked like a queen. One that took everyone's breath away and left them staring as she laughed, her blue eyes sparkling.

"It's going to match the greens in the dress perfectly, and it's exactly what you need." Sophia held the box out to Liv.

She tensed as she opened the lid, revealing the necklace she hadn't laid eyes on in many, many years.

It was more beautiful than she remembered, with its square emeralds surrounded by sparkling diamonds. Liv's fingers pulled back before she touched it, worried that, like Inexorabilis, the gems would shock her, keeping her away.

Reading the hesitation on her face, Sophia pushed the box toward Liv. "She'd want you to wear it."

Liv shook her head. "No, she'd remember how bad I am with jewelry and tell me not to lose it."

Sophia sighed. "You're not going to lose it. And even if you did, Mommy would want you to wear it."

Her sister was right. Guinevere had often said there was no point in having nice things if you didn't use them. She didn't believe china should be locked away in a cabinet never to be used. She would have probably worn the emerald necklace more often if she'd had more occasions, but the life of a Warrior didn't provide many opportunities to go to fancy events. Thankfully, Liv thought.

"Come on," Sophia urged. "I want to see what it looks like on you."

Liv took a deep breath and picked up the necklace. It was as heavy as she'd imagined, having at least over three hundred carats of diamonds and emeralds. It exemplified incredible gnome craftsmanship and had been a gift from their father when they had their first child, Reese.

Carefully Liv slipped the necklace around her neck, fastening it in the back. Her fingers found the largest emerald on the bottom, touching it lightly as she stared down at it.

Sheepishly, she glanced up at Sophia, who let out a squeal that only dogs could hear. "It's the prettiest thing I've ever seen on you!"

Liv's cheeks flushed. "I don't know. It feels too bold. I don't think I have the right personality to pull this off."

Sophia shook her head. "Don't be crazy. You're bold, and the perfect person to wear it. No one will even be looking at the bride because you're so mesmerizing."

"Well, then, I better take it off," Liv jested. "Serena will try to murder me if I steal her thunder today."

The doorbell chimed throughout the house.

Her heart suddenly racing, Liv glanced up. "What? I'm not ready."

"Of course you are," Sophia said, bounding off the bed. "I'll go get the door."

"I'm not, though," Liv argued. "I need to—"

"You're ready," Sophia argued, running for the front door.

Liv took a last glance at herself in the mirror. If she squinted, she had to admit that she looked a bit like her mother. Guinevere Beaufont had been the most beautiful person she'd ever seen. For that matter, she was usually the most beautiful person people had ever met, including any fae. It was hard for Liv to believe she was wearing her mother's necklace and about to attend a wedding in a ball-gown. When had she grown up? It all felt a bit surreal.

Offering herself one last encouraging look, she started for the living room, taking each step carefully so as not to trip over her dress.

"I swear, Rudolf designed this dress for me just to watch me fall straight on my face," Liv said, rounding out of the bedroom.

The excited voices echoing through the loft-like room halted when Liv entered. She was pretty sure they were holding their breath, waiting for Liv to slip and fall on her ass. When she'd made it safely a few steps, she looked up victoriously.

"I did it!" Liv exclaimed.

Stefan Ludwig's mouth was partly open, his blue eyes wide with shock when he gazed at Liv from only a few feet away.

"Did what?" Sophia asked.

"I made it this far," Liv said, suddenly finding it hard to speak properly.

It was the first time Liv had seen Stefan so polished in a tuxedo. His usually chaotic hair was slicked back and parted on the side, and the rugged smile in his eyes was the perfect accessory for his ensemble.

"You're going to have to make it a lot farther in those heels," Sophia said.

Liv shook her head, realizing she couldn't go through with this under the present circumstances. "Actually, I don't." She flicked her finger at her feet and shrank an inch.

"What did you do?" Sophia asked. "Did you get rid of your heels?"

"I left them for you to play with," Liv stated, striding forward in a much more comfortable manner than before. When she was in front of Stefan, she offered him a small smile. "Are you trying to catch flies?"

He looked confused.

She pointed. "Your mouth. It's hanging open."

He slammed his lips shut, standing taller. "Well, I refuse to apologize, Warrior Beaufont. You caught me quite off-guard."

"Because you're not used to seeing me with my hair brushed?" Liv asked, restraining the laughter she always felt when bantering with Stefan. It came entirely too easy for them.

"Oh, did you brush your hair?" he asked. "I hadn't noticed. My attention was entirely stolen by—"

"The emerald necklace I'm wearing," Liv supplied. "It was my mother's."

"Uh? What?" Stefan asked, shaking his head, like in a daze. "You're wearing a necklace? Oh, that. I hardly noticed."

"Well, I get it," Liv said with a nervous sigh. "It's hard to notice much with this monstrosity of a dress I've been forced to wear."

Stefan's confused gaze flowed down her gown and then back up to her face. "Oh, dress. Yeah, I'm sorry. I didn't notice that, either. It was your—"

"Nails?" Liv supplied. "It's because I cleaned under my nails, right?"

He shook his head, hiding a smile. "No, that's not what stole my attention when you first walked into the room."

She sighed dramatically. "Hmmm. Maybe it's that I took

one of Sophia's gummy vitamins this morning. I skipped lunch, and thought that would do the trick."

Stefan's eyes didn't waver from hers as he continued to shake his head. "That's not it, Liv."

"Well, then I'm stumped," Liv said. "But we should get going. We don't want to be late. Or maybe we do. Maybe we shouldn't show up until the fae are all drunk."

"Which could take eons," Stefan offered.

"It wouldn't if they didn't day-drink every single day," Liv quipped.

"And yes, I think we ought to get going," Stefan said, offering an arm to Liv. "Do you know the way?"

She nodded, squatting first to talk to Sophia, who was teeming with excitement. "John will be up in about ten minutes after he closes the store. He said something about cooking you chicken cordon bleu and steaming some veggies. Do you know what any of those things are, or if it's safe to steam up things? I'm certain that almost all food should be fried."

Sophia and Stefan laughed. "I'm sure he'll offer me something I can eat."

Liv shook her head. "I wouldn't be so sure. But just in case, I left a bag of Cheetos in the pantry. However, you're not to eat them until you've finished the already-opened package of Sour Patch Kids."

"This is very strange household you run," Stefan said mostly to himself.

Liv shot him a mock look of offense. "It's about picking your battles." She returned her gaze to Sophia. "Please listen to John. I have movies cued up for you two on the new entertainment center." She waved to the large television she'd "installed" earlier that day.

"Is it a Disney princess movie?" Sophia asked.

Liv shook her head. "Come on. I'm not about to shove propaganda down your throat. I got you the entire *How to Train Your Dragon* series, although I'm almost certain none of the lessons will be ones you can implement with Gerald."

"Gerald?" Stefan asked, interrupting again.

Liv shot him a look. "It's her dragon's informal name."

Sophia shook her head. "No, it's not. He hasn't been named."

"But when he has," Liv stated, standing up straight, "we're going with something like Harry."

"No, we're not," Sophia said with a giggle.

"Okay, fine then. Something more literal, then. How about Scaly?" Liv asked.

Sophia pressed her little hands into Liv's side, pushing her toward the middle of the room. "Go to the wedding. And then come back. I. Can't. Wait. To. Hear. Details."

Liv gave Stefan a bored expression. "I just wished my little sister had more enthusiasm for life. She's so lackluster."

He shrugged, again offering her his arm. "Maybe there's a spell you can put on her."

Liv clutched her hand to her chest, giving him a revolted look. "You aren't insinuating that I do magic?"

"I am," he said as she took his arm, strangely enjoying his warmth. She was wearing practically nothing up top, she reasoned.

"I don't know what strange world you live in, Mr.

Ludwig, but in mine, we don't subscribe to such fantastical ideas as magic." Liv held her hand out straight and tried to remember the address for the wedding. A moment later, a portal spiraled open in the middle of the living room.

"I know. I tend to be a bit of a dreamer," Stefan said with a smile.

Liv cast a glance over her shoulder at Sophia. "I'll be home early. Please listen to John, and if you need anything—"

Her sister shook her head adamantly at her. "Go! Don't come back until you're the last one at the reception. And take tons of pictures."

Liv gave Stefan a confused expression. "What are these pictures she speaks of? And however do we take them?"

"Liv!" Sophia complained as Stefan laughed.

"Fine, and yes," Liv said, waving to her sister as they stepped through the portal. "Hold on. The commute might be a bit of a pain."

"Why?" Stefan asked, suddenly apprehensive.

Liv grinned wickedly as the portal took hold of them. "The wedding is in another dimension."

The transit through the interdimensional portal definitely wasn't as pleasant as regular ones. It made Liv's brain feel like it had been nuked in a microwave and then shoved back into her head.

When they landed, she was grateful to find her body was still the way she remembered it. However, the world around her definitely wasn't.

"Wow," Stefan said, clutching her arm tighter. "Where are we?"

"We definitely aren't in Kansas anymore, Toto," she said, looking around in awe.

"Really?" Stefan asked. "I'm the terrier in this role-playing game?"

"Not just any dog," Liv said, still taking in the strange sights around them. "You're the dog who pretty much causes all the problems, thereby starting off the story. If it wasn't for Toto, the wicked witch wouldn't have captured him, and Dorothy wouldn't have run off, and then she would have been safe during the storm, and there would be no trip to see the wizard."

"So you're saying that you're glad you brought me along, right?" Stefan asked coyly.

"I haven't decided yet," Liv replied playfully.

The sights around them could only be described as otherworldly. Liv and Stefan stood on a plane that appeared to be floating in space. The floor was semi-transparent, and under and around them, stars floated in the distance. Planets with rings and multiple moons also soared by at differing speeds.

The surface was about the size of a football field. In the distance, Liv could see a queue of fae and other magical creatures. They were lined up in front of a platinum archway that strangely seemed straight out of a science fiction novel and also quite fantastical, covered in flowers and buzzing with tiny fairies.

"I think that the ceremony is that way," Liv said, tugging Stefan in that direction.

When they were nearly to the archway, Liv realized how extraordinary the decorations were. They were floating in outer space, stars soaring by and distant planets sparkling all around them. The decorations in the strange outdoor-ish hall were quite understated. The seats were all clear, so they didn't interfere with the ability to see the precious galaxy spiraling underfoot. Standing at the front and looking quite nervous was none other than the king of the fae, Rudolf Sweetwater.

His face brightened when he saw Liv push through the crowd. He held up a hand, waving wildly at her.

She turned to the crowd at her back, looking around.

"I think he's waving for you," Stefan stated.

Liv offered him a tamed grin. "I know. It's a cute game we play."

She looked straight at Rudolf and pointed at a fae beside her. "This one?" she mouthed.

Rudolf shook his head and pointed directly at her.

She indicated Stefan. "Oh, is this who you want?"

Again Rudolf shook his head, more forcefully than before.

Liv did a three-hundred-and-sixty-degree turn, pretending to be stumped. "I don't know. Who is he pointing to?"

Stefan surprised her by taking her hand in his and leading her with impressive force down the aisle. "The king is demanding your attention."

"I know," Liv said from the side of the mouth. "I was playing with him." She tried to pull her hand from Stefan's, but he had a tight hold on her—firm but not hard.

"Oh, there you are," Rudolf said, smacking his hands on his legs with relief. He was dressed simply in a tuxedo with emerald cufflinks, and he wore a large gardenia in the lapel of his jacket. "Have you seen Liv Beaufont? She's supposed to be my best man."

Liv blinked dully at the king of the fae. "Who do you think I am?"

"Well, you're the double she sent to fool me," he answered. "I'm looking for the real thing." He brought his hand down to mid-chest. "She's about this high, and usually has a rat's nest in her hair and dirty smudges on her face. Have you seen her?"

Liv lowered her chin. "I'm the real deal."

His eyes widened. "Nooooo."

"Oh, yes, King Dumbface. It's me."

He opened his arms wide and, without asking permission, wrapped them around her. "It *is* you. Only Liv would call me by that adorable nickname."

"If you don't take your hands off me, I'm going to toss you off of this floating plane in the middle of space," Liv said through clenched teeth.

Rudolf pulled back with a laugh. "And I see you were able to find a date. How much?" He indicated to Stefan.

Liv blinked dully at him. "I didn't hire a male escort."

Looking Stefan over carefully, Rudolf nodded appreciatively. "No, I see that he isn't male now. But he almost had me fooled. Anyway, it doesn't matter to me whether you prefer male or female hookers. The point is that you found someone who would tolerate you."

"And right there, you pretty much stole half my speech for the toast." Liv sighed.

"In all seriousness," Rudolf said, pulling Liv in closer like he wanted a black eye for the ceremony. "Where are the rings?"

Liv leaned in closer. "In all seriousness, what the hell are you talking about?"

"Well, I told you to bring the rings for the ceremony," he said tersely, looking over his shoulder as more guests took their seats.

"Ru, did you tell me this directly or through the imaginary link you think we have?" Liv asked him.

He leveled his chin and grinned. "I don't think I have to answer that."

Liv threw her hands into the air. "Seriously, you don't have rings for the ceremony?"

"Well, that depends," Rudolf began. "Did you bring them?"

"No, because you didn't tell me to."

"I did so."

"You did not."

"Yes, I did."

Stefan stepped between the two of them, momentarily pausing them. "Maybe now isn't the time for blame."

"I think now is the perfect time for blame," Liv stated. "Then we progress to violence, followed by more insults, and then we finish off with headlocks."

Stefan pressed his fingers into Liv's arm, and the effect was strange. She suddenly felt much calmer. It was easier to breathe, whereas moments prior, her chest had felt constricted. "Is there a way to conjure up some rings?"

"I don't think so," Liv stated. "We are in a different dimension because *someone* just had to have a destination wedding." She glanced over Stefan's shoulder at the groom.

"It was this or an Elvis wedding, and we both know I can't be upstaged by a man with better hair than me," Rudolf stated.

"Liv, there has to be a way to find some rings here," Stefan said, sounding like the only voice of reason in the entire universe.

Absentmindedly, Liv glanced around the hall, hoping that the bright attire of the guests would inspire her. That was when she noticed two giants strolling into the hall. "Rory!"

She pulled away from Rudolf and Stefan, hurrying toward Rory and Bermuda at the front.

"Okay, we'll take a five-minute break while you think over options," Rudolf called as Liv departed.

Rory and Bermuda stood taller than the crowd who was filing to their seats. Liv squeezed through the fae and found Rory's hand, tugging on it.

"Mum, I think I got bitten on the hand by something on the way over here," Rory said, looking at his mother, although Liv was plainly in view for them both to see.

"It was probably one of the flies. They are pesky little things," Bermuda replied.

"Hey, guys!" Liv said, tugging even harder on the giant's hand. "It's me! Liv!"

Rory glanced around like he had heard something but couldn't quite place the source. "Mum, do you hear anything?"

Bermuda played along with the act. She was wearing a sequined blue gown and large hat with a peacock on it. Rory was wearing the suit he'd donned for Rudolf's coronation. "I heard a sound like a sheep being slaughtered, but that's about it."

"Hey, guys!" Liv yelled, trying to get their attention over the crowd filing to their seats.

"There's that noise again," Bermuda said. "It is like nails on a chalkboard, isn't it?"

"Ha-ha," Liv said, releasing Rory's hand. "Fine, I'm not happy you are alive, I don't need your help to save the ceremony, and I'm going to go and launch myself over the side of this precarious plane floating in outer space."

Rory glanced down at Liv, his face brightening. "Oh, there you are. Why didn't you say you were here?"

Liv let out a long breath. "I didn't realize you had time to enroll in clown college while you were gone. You really should get your money back."

"What's this about needing help saving the ceremony?" Bermuda asked, sliding into the spot next to her son.

Liv bowed. "It's lovely to see you, too. I'd kiss you on either cheek, which is customary for the giants—"

"It's not," Bermuda interrupted.

"But I don't have a ladder," Liv continued, not missing a beat.

"Is everything okay?" Rory asked her.

"Shouldn't I be asking you two that?" Liv questioned.

"Yes, and it's fine," Rory stated. "We will fill you in later."

"Decar?" Liv asked.

"Later," he hissed.

"Okay, fine," Liv stated. "Anyway, I need two rings really quickly. Can you forge something?"

"Ummm, no," Rory said. "I don't have…well, any equipment or materials, and there a are a ton of fae around."

"Okay, well, too bad," Liv sang. "I'll just tell Rudolf that—"

"The rings are for the king of the fae?" Bermuda asked. "Who was responsible for them? The best man, I presume."

"Yes, but that idiot totally forgot them," Liv said dismissively. "We'll call it a communications snafu."

Bermuda pursed her lips. "That man should be booted out of this wedding. That's atrocious."

"I agree," Liv stated. "I think that person should totally

leave here and be able to spend the rest of their night in yoga pants on the couch watching cartoons."

Bermuda and Rory gave her curious glances.

"You're the best man, aren't you?" Rory asked.

"Yes, but I was never told to bring rings," Liv stated.

"It's common knowledge that the best man brings the rings," Bermuda said smugly.

"Well, it appears that my education on how to be a proper best man was neglected," Liv said. "Is there anything I can do? Can we just improvise?"

"I'm afraid not," Bermuda said, combing her large hand over her sturdy chin as she thought. "The rings that the fae use in this ceremony are meant to bond them for life."

"But does it really matter since the bride is an airhead mortal?" Liv asked, gaining the attention of a few fae filing to their seats. "I meant that as a compliment."

The fae didn't seem to believe her, and they turned away.

"Oh, really, Liv," Bermuda said, opening her large purse. "How do you get yourself into these situations?"

"The short answer is that I was born," she replied.

From her purse, Bermuda pulled out two silver balls. "These would work, although we have nothing to forge them with."

Liv grabbed the two balls from her hand and darted for the back, where she'd just seen two other familiar faces enter.

"You're welcome, Warrior Beaufont," Bermuda called through the crowd.

"Put it on my tab," Liv called over her shoulder, sliding through the tight cluster of fae. She stopped when at a particularly crowded area, pushing people aside. "Out of the way. Father Time isn't taking requests right now. This is a social affair."

The fae she nearly pushed over gave her looks of offense until they saw it was her. Most of them dispersed when she came to stand in front of Subner and Father Time.

Liv glanced over her shoulder at the gnomes, surveying the area. "I didn't expect you two here."

"We were obligated," Father Time said.

"Didn't you think that a bodyguard would be in order?" Liv asked, continuing to give fae dirty looks who appeared like they wanted to make a request of Papa Creola.

"Well, with the newbies you hired recently, we thought requests would be down," Father Time stated.

Liv huffed. "Those are formal requests. There will always be the rogue fae or magical creature who doesn't want to make a formal request but sees you out in public and decides to be ballsy. Just wait until the champagne starts flowing around here."

Papa Creola glanced briefly at Subner. "It appears I should have come in costume."

A moment later, the jovial gnome took the shape of a female fae wearing a silver ball gown that had a slit all the way up. The shimmering sparkles of the sexy dress matched the fae's wings.

"Dang," Liv said with a whistle. "When you go incognito, you go all the way."

"What can I say? I like to express my feminine side when I can," Papa Creola said, batting his long eyelashes before striding off for his seat.

Liv rounded on Subner. "Hey, I need a really quick favor. Can you please turn these into rings?" She opened the palm of her hand to show the two silver balls.

The gnome regarded the objects in her hand and then laughed. "You want me to magically just transform those into sacred bands that will bond the king of the fae to his wife for the rest of their lives?"

Liv peered down at the balls and then nodded. "Can you?"

"Are those pieces of silver from the Isle of Man where giants excavate their metals?" Subner asked.

Liv's eyes skirted to the left and the right. "I guess so. Why?"

"No reason," he said and snatched up the two balls, seamlessly leaving two shiny rings behind in Liv's hand.

Her mouth fell open, and then it all added up for her. "Wait, you and Papa Creola knew I'd need rings, didn't you?"

He pocketed the balls of silver. "Maybe."

"And you wanted giant silver, didn't you?" she continued to ask.

"Does it really matter?" Subner asked, striding after the tall blonde fae at the front of the hall who looked nothing like Papa Creola. "You have your rings, and that's all that matters, right?"

Liv grunted in affirmation, realizing that she was sweating from the impromptu mission. "Why even on my day off am I having to babysit fae and fix ridiculous problems?"

## CHAPTER TWENTY-SIX

There had been so many surprises on that day, but the biggest one was the sight of Serena. When the mortal entered the hall with Saturn visible in the distance and dazzling stars all around her, she was the most beautiful thing in the universe.

It proved to Liv that fae didn't have the market cornered on beauty. Serena was and would always be mortal, but she was absolutely gorgeous, and Rudolf loved her. And that meant there were many other ways mortals could intertwine with magical creatures' lives, saving both their hearts and their magic.

Stoically, Liv stood beside Rudolf as his bride took the long trail up to him. Liv's eyes roamed over the crowd, astonished by all the various faces. She winked at Rory, who looked uncomfortable in his suit. Bermuda had a tissue pressed to her nose like she was ready to start crying at any moment. Papa Creola appeared absolutely ravishing as a female fae, and beside him, Subner mostly seemed bored. However, the fact that the two were there was pretty amazing.

As Liv surveyed the large audience, she realized that all eyes were centered on the bride as she made her way to the front. Well, all sets of eyes except one.

Stefan Ludwig was looking straight at Liv.

She widened her eyes at him when she noticed that, covertly pointing at the place in front of her where Serena would soon be.

Minutely, Stefan shook his head, an act of real defiance.

Liv rolled her eyes, deciding to scold him later for his disobedience.

Although Liv had worried that Rudolf and Serena would make a debacle of their ceremony, it was actually quite tame. The whole thing lasted less than half an hour, and when it was time to hand over the rings, Liv was grateful she had two to supply Rudolf with.

He gave her an appreciative nod before taking them. When it was time to seal the deal with a kiss, the entire congregation erupted in applause. Many of those in the wedding party had big white flowers bloom on their clothes. Liv glanced down but didn't see anything different.

She shook her head, realizing it was going to take a lot more than an otherworldly union of the king of the fae with a dead mortal to spark the love in her heart.

"And now, it is my prestigious honor to present to you for the first time ever," the priest conducting the ceremony finished, "King and Queen Sweetwater."

Shimmering dust rained down from the heavens, covering the tops of heads as Rudolf and Serena sped off for the back. Liv followed the happy couple, amazed by the lavish things people did to express their love. She didn't understand it, and yet, she was completely in awe of anything so powerful.

---

Never having been a part of a wedding party, Liv wasn't used to the attention she got during the reception. It was held in the area in front of the ceremony. Apparently, Rudolf had negotiated with the centaurs to have falling stars for the night's festivities. It wasn't a planned one, which meant a few thousand stars were going to die that night for no reason other than the fact that their burning through space made for beautiful decorations for the festivities.

Liv had wrung a hundred hands it seemed, pretending to smile as fae commented on her dress or how she made a very nice best man. She nodded politely, wishing it was time for cake.

"What an unexpected surprise," a squeaky voice said in front of Liv.

She glanced around, looking for the source, seeing only the backs of heads and laughing fae not paying any attention to her.

"Down here, Liv Beaufont, Warrior for the House of Seven."

Liv looked down to find Mortimer the brownie waving at her. Beside her was his secretary Pricilla, wearing an oversized gown that made her look…bigger.

"Mortimer and Pricilla!" Liv exclaimed, grateful to finally see someone she knew. "I'm glad to see you here."

"You as well," Mortimer said, bowing slightly to her. He was much trimmer than she'd ever seen him. His hair was thicker on his head and missing from his ears and neck. "We have news."

"Oh?" Liv asked, kneeling down so she was closer to the height of the brownies. "Does this have to do with the official office?"

Mortimer gave a sneaky grin to Pricilla. "Maybe. We will be taking off a little more time in the future."

"Because you're expanding operations?" Liv asked.

He shook his head.

"Because you're attending safety training?" Liv questioned.

Again he shook his head. "No, Liv Beaufont, we are going to be welcoming a new member of our family."

"Oh, wow!" Liv exclaimed. "That's wonderful news."

"Well, we didn't know if you knew we were an item," Mortimer said, blushing. "It was because of many of our discussions that I asked Pricilla out. And since then, well, things have progressed."

Liv winked. "I'd say. Please let me know what you two will be needing. I'd love to send a gift."

Mortimer waved as Pricilla dragged him toward the buffet, overflowing with the most decadent foods. "Will do! Thank you, Liv Beaufont."

---

Never before had Liv addressed so many people. She held up her champagne flute, giving Rudolf an uncertain smile. He appeared eager for her speech, as was Serena beside him—or at least she was getting better at suppressing her sneer.

Glancing out at the audience, ready for her speech, Liv felt her dinner ready to crawl up her throat.

"Ummm..." she began, the nervousness bouncing around inside her stomach. It was astonishing to her that she could face down giant beetles and many other villains, but speaking publicly made her want to vomit.

The crowd began to whisper among themselves, obviously put off by Liv's less than stellar speech.

"The first time I met Rudolf Sweetwater," Liv finally said in a rush, diverting from her planned and rehearsed speech, "he refused to help me because he said he needed proof of my noble mission before helping me."

The crowd all gave Liv their attention, expectant expressions on their faces.

Liv cleared her throat. "I thought he was a laffy-taffy who had broken out of the mental hospital for magical disorders." She looked around at the crowd. "Actually, I'm wondering right now if many of you worked together for a massive breakout."

The audience laughed.

"However, as I got to know Rudolf, I realized he wasn't insane. Well, he is, but not just crazy. I was there when this man defeated Visa. I was there when he risked everything, including my life, to steal the resurrection stone from Father Time. I was there when he revived Serena. And all of these experiences have left me with a very solid conclusion."

Liv revolved her gaze around the audience, enjoying

that everyone was now leaning forward, hanging on what she would say next.

"Yes, Rudolfus Sweetwater is a ridiculous and sometimes irritating individual who will do whatever it takes to get what he wants," Liv began, "but he is also a wonderful person who will do absolutely anything for the people he loves. He wouldn't help me until he knew I was good. He didn't stop until the woman he loved was back on this Earth. Well, not *this* Earth, since I have absolutely no idea where we are, but the Earth we come from, which I think is over there somewhere." Liv pointed randomly. "And I'll tell you that Rudolf didn't hesitate for a single second when facing Visa. He put his life on the line, knowing that if he conquered that evil queen, the fae would benefit."

Liv raised her glass, giving Rudolf a fond expression. "You are a lot of things, Ru. Annoying, slightly brain-dead, poorly educated, badly mannered, and sometimes—"

From the front row of the audience, next to Stefan, Rory coughed loudly, indiscreetly saying, "Your point?"

"Right," Liv said, straightening. "My point is that I might not be the typical best man, but I'm honored to raise a glass to someone I consider to be one of the best fae kings to reign. Rudolf and Serena, I wish you the very best. Everyone should have a love that transcends death and intelligence, just like you two."

The audience erupted in applause, clinking their glasses and drinking. Automatically their glasses were refilled to the brim as the band began playing.

Rudolf and Serena took the middle of the floor for their first dance as everyone watched in awe.

Liv took a sip of her champagne, grateful that her job

was finally done for the night. Now she could go back to wrestling bad men and risking her life for magic, a job that was much easier than speaking in front of a crowd.

"Your face," Stefan said at her side.

Liv pretended like his sudden appearance hadn't startled her. "My face what?"

He studied her expression for a moment. "Earlier, when I picked you up, and you wondered what had me in awe?"

"Oh, this ridiculous dress," she said, looking down at the magicked material, which kept shifting from dark greens to light pinks.

He shook his head, offering his hand to her. "May I please have this dance, Ms. Liv Beaufont?"

Terror raced around in her mind, screaming that she should run through a burning building first, or maybe try to hunt down a deranged three-headed dragon.

"I promise you I don't bite," Stefan said, having sensed her apprehension.

With no way to refuse, Liv took his hand, allowing him to lead her onto the dance floor. Once enfolded in his arms, he effortlessly led them across the space, dancing with a grace she'd had no idea he possessed.

"You can actually dance," Liv said, staring over Stefan's shoulder.

"There are a lot of things about me you don't know," he said in a teasing voice.

"Like what?" Liv asked.

"Well, my favorite ice cream flavor is cookies and cream, pineapple on pizza should be outlawed, and Eggs Benedict is the only real breakfast food."

"Anything that doesn't involve your dietary preferences?" Liv asked.

"Is there anything else you need to know about a person?"

She shrugged. "Not really."

"I have a question for you," Stefan said, twirling Liv around the dance floor, a strange elegance to his movements. It was like when he was on the battlefield racing after demons, but softer. Meant for her. And it was perfect.

"Blue," she said at once, trying to cover her sudden nervousness

He shook his head. "I don't want to know your favorite color."

"Eight," she supplied.

"Nor your favorite number."

She huffed. "That shows how much you know. That's the number of men I've killed."

He laughed. "No, it's not."

"Yeah, you're right, it's not."

Stefan dipped her slightly, suddenly serious. "Liv, I know you're working on something separate from House business. You don't have to tell me, but you can trust me if you want to."

Liv stood and parted from Stefan, suddenly put off balance by his request. He hadn't pushed her, and yet that was exactly what it felt like. Deep inside, she knew he could be trusted, but she couldn't tell him about the House of Fourteen. Before, she hadn't wanted to put him in danger. Now that she knew a Beaufont was the only one who spread the information and it would make the person take up the cause, it was even harder. Stefan was already governed by a curse that made him tirelessly fight evil. How could she burden him any further?

However, as she peered deep into his blue eyes, she realized two things simultaneously. First, she respected Stefan Ludwig almost more than anyone else in the world. He hadn't blindly asked for trust. He'd earned it. Time and time again, in the silent moments of battle together, in the dark hours when nightmares became real as they fought beasts, Stefan had proven through his actions that no matter what, he'd never let her down.

The other realization was so much subtler, and yet just as powerful. Stefan Ludwig, whether he was a friend or someone much closer to Liv, he deserved to know about the House of Fourteen.

Liv glided her hand down until it met his. Then she pulled him away from the crowd and told him everything.

## CHAPTER TWENTY-SEVEN

The upgraded signal had been broadcasting for twenty-four hours.

That should have been enough time.

Adler Sinclair paced, his robe tangling between his legs.

Something was wrong. He knew it. He'd never been one to trust instincts; those were pesky emotions that proved nothing. However, he couldn't shake the strange feeling in his stomach, as though something that had been connected to him for a long time was gone. Missing. Vacant.

But that was impossible. *We aren't all connected like dumb hippies like to think*, Adler thought. Everyone was alone, trying to make the best of the circumstances they were placed in. Currently, Adler needed to know what the signal was doing. He stopped himself from tweaking it. Changing things. Instead, he just continued to pace, waiting.

The ring of the phone in his pocket nearly made him jump.

Scrambling, Adler pulled his phone from his pocket,

and it nearly fell out of his hands when he placed it to his ear.

"What?" he barked into the receiver.

"Sir?" the woman's voice said.

"Yes, what?"

"It's working," she reported, not needing to say more.

"Are you sure?" he asked.

"Yes. An epidemic has befallen North America's largest cities," the woman reported. "Thousands are dying."

Adler hung up, smiling for the first time in what felt like forever.

He had done it. Mortals would soon be extinct.

## CHAPTER TWENTY-EIGHT

"Wow, I knew it," Stefan said when Liv had finished telling him everything.

She regarded him with a look of pure disbelief for a full ten seconds. Then she slapped him on the arm. "No, you didn't."

He laughed, catching her hand and holding it. "No, Liv, I didn't. But wow! That's crazy." Shaking his head, his blue eyes grew larger. "Only you could have uncovered this."

"It was my destiny," she explained. "Beaufonts are meant to find this information. It's what killed my parents, my siblings, and who knows who else."

With a somber look, Stefan nodded. "And you told *me*. I'm really grateful for that. We have a lot of work to do."

Her first instinct was to tell him to stay out of it, that this was her business. However, since she had decided to bring Stefan into things, she had to allow him to help. And if she was honest with herself, she was relieved to know he was part of it now. She didn't want to put him in danger, but she did want to win this. That seemed more likely with Stefan on her side.

Staring out at the stars, Liv watched with Stefan as stars streaked across the inky darkness. She tried to make a new wish every time one rocketed by, but they fell with such quickness, it was hard to keep up.

"Are you counting stars?" Stefan asked, and Liv realized that as she watched the stars, he was watching her.

"Stop looking at me like that just because I'm wearing a dumb dress," she scolded.

He laughed. "You've got me all wrong. I'm not looking at you because you're wearing a dress or your hair is brushed or your sister painted your face." Stefan leaned close. "I actually prefer you in a cape and boots with a sword at your side."

"Stop sucking up, Ludwig," Liv said, pulling away slightly.

"It's true," he said, yanking her back in close.

To her horror, a dumb-ass giggle escaped Liv's mouth. She couldn't believe it. She'd giggled. Whoever had spiked her drink was going to die. But as she looked at Stefan, she did feel strangely giddy.

"Do you prefer me as a warrior?" Stefan asked.

Liv took a step back, checking out his smart tuxedo. "I don't know. I could get used to seeing you in tails."

Stefan gracefully found her hand in a swift movement that would have gone unnoticed by most. He moved like the wind, a gift he had stolen from demons and used for the good of the Warriors. Twirling her out and then back into him, he caught her with his other hand.

"What did you wish for, Liv?" he whispered beside her head.

She closed her eyes, not wanting to allow herself this moment but needing it more than she knew.

"A happy ending," she answered honestly.

If her eyes had been open, she would have seen her dress blossom all over, making her appear to be a spring garden where love was allowed to flourish.

## CHAPTER TWENTY-NINE

Liv and Stefan stood staring at the falling stars for a long time.

Finally, he said, "I never took you as the type to wish."

"I just thought it couldn't hurt," she stated.

"Well, I have a whole bag of coins for you to throw into that fountain in your house," he said, a laugh in his voice.

She wiggled out of his arms, feigning an expression of fury. "Oh, don't you mock me, Mr. Ludwig."

"I wouldn't dream of it, Ms. Beaufont," he replied, bowing to her. "So what's next? How do we return it to the House of Fourteen?" Stefan asked, looking around at the display of planets and stars.

"I keep following the clues," she said. "I've got to find Adler."

"Speaking of following clues," Rory said, interrupting them.

Liv turned around to find the giant standing next to his mum Bermuda. "Hey."

Rory glanced around the area. There was no one else

around, most being off dancing. From his large suit jacket, Rory pulled a book. "This is what Mum recovered."

Liv took the book, finding it much heavier than she expected. "Wow, what are these pages made out of? Lead?"

"Paper, dear Liv," Bermuda corrected, not appearing amused.

"Oh, sorry," Liv said unapologetically. "I totally thought the book was made of metal."

Rory gave his mother a sideways glance. "No, she didn't."

"Do either of you want to tell me what's going on?" She indicated Stefan. "He can be trusted."

"Of course, he can," Bermuda said. "That was why you just told him the secret that only a Beaufont can pass along."

Liv gave the giant a dumbfounded expression. "How do you know…Never mind. I'm chalking it all up to voodoo at this point."

Bermuda pointed to the book in Liv's hands. "That's the *Forgotten Archive*. Once you activate it, the real history, the one everyone was forced to forget, will automatically take over. However, it's important that mortals can see magic first. Otherwise, they will question the new history. The timing of everything is important."

Liv studied the book, which appeared completely normal. "I can't believe this is the solution. I just have to make mortals see magic again."

"Believe me when I say that I had the easy job," Bermuda stated.

"That reminds me," Liv said, handing the book to

Stefan. He gave her a questioning glance. "Does it look like I've got pockets in this dress?"

He nodded at once and slipped the book into his pocket.

"What happened to Decar?" Liv asked the giants.

They exchanged looks. "Although we preferred for it not to come to this, we ended up having to battle just before arriving here. He wouldn't let up on us," Bermuda explained.

"He's dead now," Rory said.

Liv didn't feel better knowing this. The death of ones' enemies didn't bring peace. It simply reminded them of the horrible things they faced, that death was even an option.

"But you two are safe," Liv said in a hushed voice. "I'm grateful for that."

"And now you must go and see Rudolf," Bermuda told her. "He has asked for you."

Liv looked over her shoulder at the party going on behind them. "Rudolf? But he's…"

"He needs you," Rory urged.

Liv nodded, seeing the severity of their expressions. "Okay." She turned to face Stefan, but he seemed to already sense what she needed to hear.

"I'll keep the book safe and be here when you return," he stated. "Then we'll head back together."

Liv pushed through the crowd, trying to make her way to the front. The drunker the fae got, the harder it was to convince them that she needed to get through the crowd and didn't want to dance.

She was almost to the front when Liv noticed a familiar face she hadn't expected to see there. "Emilio?"

The Warrior turned around, parting from a beautiful fae with long black hair. He wore a guilty expression and entirely too much cologne.

"What are you doing here?" Liv questioned.

Furiously, he shook his head. "You can't tell my sister. I didn't think you'd notice me."

Liv gave him an incredulous glare. "You are one of three magicians here, and you didn't think I'd notice you?"

Grabbing her arm in a very rude manner, he tried to tug her away. Liv yanked her arm back but followed, sensing the urgency he was feeling.

When they were far enough from the crowd, Emilio turned to her. "I'm in love with a fae."

"Are you sure you don't have an STD?" Liv asked.

He shook his head. "No. I know they can play mind games and spread strange…"

"Diseases," Liv said. "That's the word you're looking for."

"It's not that, though," Emilio said. "We're in love. And we want to be together."

"Congrats," Liv said, searching the crowd for Rudolf. "I'll be at the wedding. I already have a dress."

Again the Warrior shook his head. "You don't understand. Bianca has forbidden me to date a fae. She's told me it's a betrayal."

"Has she looked in the mirror?" Liv asked. "Those high-collared dresses she wears make me feel like I'm suffocating."

Emilio didn't seem to be in the mood to laugh. "As the elder, she can replace me with one of our younger cousins. She says that if I marry a fae, I'll muddy the Mantovani bloodline. If she finds out, then—"

"First off," Liv began, "you're at a wedding reception for a fae and a mortal. And not just any fae, I'll remind you. The king of the fae. He's not worried about muddying his bloodline, although I'm certain he's not operating with a great genetic pool anyway."

"Bianca won't care," Emilio stated. "She's adamant that I not be with anyone who isn't a magician. She especially hates mortals."

Liv let out a long breath. "I'm not surprised. And don't worry, your secret is safe with me."

He sighed in relief. "Thank you."

"But this isn't over," Liv stated with conviction. "When I have time, which I'm not sure when that will be, I'll be remedying this issue. I'm tired of living in a segregated magical world."

"But the House is only powerful as long as our bloodlines are pure," Emilio stated.

Liv shook her head. "That's what they want us to believe. The House was never about blood. We're about justice."

It took Liv another ten minutes to find Rudolf. He wasn't on the dance floor, as she expected. He wasn't licking the chocolate fountain, either. To her surprise, his security brought her to a private area where he was seated beside Serena, who lay on a bed, her forehead sweating profusely.

"What is it?" Liv asked him.

He shook his head. "She's fallen sick."

"Why?" Liv asked, studying the area for clues. "Is it the dimension? Elevation sickness? Did she eat plastic again?"

"I don't think so," Rudolf stated. He stood, glancing thoughtfully at his wife. "I've had reports from Earth."

That was a strange thing to say, but Liv kept her quip locked away.

"Apparently mortals are growing sick all over the world," Rudolf explained. "I'm not sure why. Maybe there's a disease they are falling prey to. I also wanted to bring something else to your attention."

"Yes?" Liv asked, her heart suddenly beating wildly.

Rudolf pointed to a decanter on the table beside Serena's bed. It was filled halfway with bubbling champagne.

"Wow, that's super impressive," Liv said with zero inflection in her voice.

He shook his head. "You don't get it. I just tried to fill that decanter all the way up with champagne. It's been like that all night. My magic...it isn't at full power anymore... for some reason."

Liv took a step back, piecing it all together. Serena hadn't caught some disease. Rudolf's magic wasn't ill. The two were connected, and she suspected that Adler was behind this. Magic was at risk because mortals were ill.

The end was coming soon unless she put a stop to it.

## CHAPTER THIRTY

Clark turned the *Forgotten Archives* over in his hand, a cautious expression on his face. "I want to go with you."

Liv's eyes drifted to Stefan, who was propped up in the corner. He'd exchanged his tuxedo for his usual all-black outfit and cape. She'd also changed as soon as she'd returned home.

"You know you can't," Liv stated. "If something happens to me—"

"Nothing will happen to you," Stefan cut in.

She gave him a confident nod and returned her gaze to Clark. "I know you want to go with me, but someone has to look after Sophia."

The young magician was asleep on the couch next to John, her head on his lap as he gently combed his fingers through her hair.

Clark threw his arm at the pair. "John is looking after her."

"No," Liv said deliberately. "I mean if I don't return."

"Liv," Stefan said, an edge in his voice.

"There's a real possibility that I won't return," Liv fired. "My parents died on the Matterhorn."

"Because Adler cheated and locked their magic," he argued.

"It doesn't matter," Liv replied. "We don't know what dangers we'll face up there. If you're going with me, then you've got to know this could be the most dangerous mission we've faced."

"I *am* going with you," he stated with authority.

"Why does Stefan get to go with you but I don't?" Clark said, sounding a bit childish.

She understood, though. Sitting at home while she and Stefan took out evil bruised Clark's ego. It would hers, too. But he wasn't trained for this. He was a Councilor. That was what they did. They stayed behind while Warriors faced down evil and exterminated it.

"Stefan and I work well together," she said, keeping her eyes off the other Warrior. Things had shifted between them during the wedding reception. There was no going back to how things had been, and she was absolutely fine with that. Actually, if she were honest with herself, what she had with Stefan was exactly what she wanted. Someone strong at her side. An equal. A relationship that she was proud of. A man she craved. A romance that had the possibility of rivaling her parents'.

"But his magic could be locked," Clark argued.

"Adler doesn't suspect him. It's the Beaufonts he's worried about," Liv said in a convincing tone.

"Well, what am I supposed to do with this?" Clark asked, holding up the book.

"Read it," Liv stated. "That's the real history. Once the signal is shut off, we can activate the real history so that everyone remembers it. But for now, you have to keep it safe. Maybe there's something in there that can help us."

"Yeah, you don't even know what you're up against, or how you're going to shut down the signal," Clark said, still trying to make a case for why he should go.

"I might be able to help with that," John said, speaking up for the first time since they'd started this meeting. "Alicia and I have been discussing this signal business."

The scientist had asked a lot of questions when Liv had asked her to help with unregistering her magic. She trusted Alicia, but she didn't want to burden her the same way she had Stefan. That was why she had told her what she thought was relevant to her, which was the signal broadcasting from the Matterhorn.

Carefully, John moved Sophia off of his lap and stood up. "I couldn't figure out what sort of signal could be broadcasting from the Matterhorn that was so powerful it could affect mortals worldwide. However, Alicia explained how magic tech works, and that got me to thinking. Shutting something of that caliber down won't be easy. It's not like flipping a switch since it's magically fueled."

From his back pocket, he pulled out what appeared to be a jump drive. "Alicia and I made this. It's a virus of sorts. If you plug it into the electronic power supply of whatever is broadcasting the signal, it should corrupt the magic aspect and thereby bring down the entire thing."

Liv's face lit up. "That's genius, John. Thank you. I was just going to blow up whatever the source was."

"And possible yourself, and a much-loved mountain," John replied, handing over the device.

"Good thinking," Liv said, feeling a tender fondness for the man before her. John had been there for her all these years. He wasn't just the reason her magic was stronger, since he was a Mortal Seven. He was the reason *she* was strong.

Before she could stop herself, Liv threw her arms around his shoulders, hugging him tightly. He seemed surprised by the gesture but recovered quickly and wrapped his arms around her. When she pulled away, he was smiling thoughtfully at her.

"You'll be back, Liv," John stated with enthusiasm.

"Of course I will," Liv assured him. "And then I'm taking you to the House of Fourteen. There's a spot on the council with your name on it. But first, you take that vacation you had to postpone."

"Yes. It will be quite different once mortals are back in the fold," Clark said, standing as well.

"It will be better," Liv asserted with conviction.

"So you're really going to do this, then?" Clark asked, fidgeting with the book.

Liv saw the worry in his features, but there was little she could say to relieve his fears. She was about to take the same path her parents had before they died. She'd almost died on the Matterhorn too. If it hadn't been for Plato, she would have.

But she hadn't. And she wasn't planning on dying that day or anytime soon.

"I'll be in touch with you as soon as I have an update," Liv stated.

"On that silly pad of paper you gave me?" Clark asked.

"It's an anywhere pad," she corrected. "Alicia suspects that devices, even magical tech ones, won't work on the Matterhorn due to the signal. If you need to tell me something, use that."

"And what do you want me to tell Sophia when she wakes up?" Clark asked, indicating the sweet girl asleep on the couch.

"Tell her the truth," Liv stated, striding over the sofa. "And tell her that I'll be back as soon as I'm done."

She leaned over and laid a soft kiss on Sophia's forehead.

"And please stop making her drink those disgusting green shakes for breakfast," Liv said to her brother. "She hates them, but is too polite to tell you."

"They are good for her," Clark argued, a small grin hiding in his eyes.

"So is laughing," Liv argued. "Make her laugh instead."

He shook his head but seemed compliant to her requests as he opened his arms to her.

"What are you doing?" Liv asked, giving him a skeptical expression.

"I'm going to give you a hug before you leave," he stated.

She shook her head. "No, that's not necessary."

Clark appeared hurt. "But you hugged John."

"That's because he made some magic tech that will help our mission."

"And you kissed Sophia," Clark continued.

"Because she's a sweet little angel," Liv reasoned. "If I hug you, it's going to seem like we're afraid I'm not returning, and that's not the message I want to put out to the universe."

"But Liv, what if—"

"Oh, fine, then," Liv said and closed the distance between them, folding Clark into her arms. He pressed her head into his chest, and she could feel his fear radiating off him.

If she gave herself the chance, she'd feel it too. But worries were better left behind for the journey she was taking. They would only make her weak.

## CHAPTER THIRTY-ONE

The weather wasn't any better than the first time Liv had been on the Matterhorn. It wasn't any worse, either. It was different…

She couldn't place why the air seemed strange. It was like the wind was blowing in the wrong direction.

"So you and the demon hunter," Plato said once she'd stepped through the portal and oriented herself on the trail up the Matterhorn.

"Yeah," she said proudly. "I like him. Sue me."

"I don't think people throw lawsuits at others anymore for their affections," Plato said.

"But they used to?" Liv asked.

"Back in the fourteenth century, you could get sued for looking at someone the wrong way."

Liv glanced back at the portal, wondering what was taking Stefan so long to come through.

"I might have stalled his arrival," Plato said guiltily.

"Why would you do that?" Liv asked, then shook her head. "And how?"

"Portal magic is sort of my specialty."

"Why did you stall him?" Liv asked.

"So I could tell you something," Plato admitted.

Liv stared up at the summit ahead of her, preparing herself for what came next. "I'll be careful. Don't worry."

"I'm not worried," he said. "But I do have a confession to make."

Liv lowered her chin and scowled at the lynx. "You *did* eat the last of the cookie dough, didn't you?"

"No," Plato stated. "I threw it away. That stuff has MSG in it."

"When did you become so health conscious?"

"Since I realized you don't have nine lives," Plato said with an uncharacteristic bit of force to his tone.

Liv reeled back, surprised by his strange behavior. "Is everything okay?"

"It will be," he said, an air of mystery in his voice.

"Okay, this confession you have…"

"I have two actually," he began. "The first I'll tell you now. The other one, well, it will have to wait until later."

"Then why even tell me there are two?" she asked.

"Because much like me, you're driven by curiosity."

"So you think that if I know there's some secret you're going to reveal to me, I'll have extra motivation to live and return from this mission? Is that right?"

Plato nodded. "And also, I'm not ready to tell you the other one. I need more time."

"To do what?" Liv asked.

"To figure things out," he said simply.

"Okay, so what *can* you tell me?"

"Liv, do you remember when we met?"

"How could I not?" she said, studying the landscape. It was the ideal time to hike the Matterhorn. There wasn't much snow, and the conditions were right, except for that strange wind she still didn't understand.

"It was the day after your parents died and you left the House of Seven, abdicating your role as Warrior," Plato stated.

"Yes, I remember it like it was yesterday."

"I knew your parents before you and I met," Plato confessed.

"You what?" Liv asked, not sure why this surprised her. It was just that her best friend had never told her, and it really seemed like something he should have mentioned.

"It's true," he said, nodding. "Your parents, well, they had done me a few favors over the years."

"Favors?" Liv asked.

"Mostly got me out of some jams," Plato explained.

"You're acting like they got your parking tickets dismissed."

"Magical parking tickets, if you will," Plato said casually. "Anyway, in return, they asked me to watch out for one of their children if anything should ever happen to them."

And just like that, everything Liv thought she knew in the world crashed down around her. If she'd been holding anything, she would have dropped it. If she'd been sitting, she would have fallen out of her chair. If her heart hadn't already been fractured, it would have broken. Her knees softened, and she focused on staying upright. "You're only here out of obligation."

"No," he said at once. "I originally showed up out of obligation. However, I've stayed because I've wanted to.

My agreement with your parents was that I stay until you took on your role as Warrior, if that should ever happen."

"Why are you telling me this?" Liv asked, feeling slightly less fragile. For years, she'd wondered why Plato had shown up when he did. She'd worried about questioning him on the subject, concerned she might push him away. Actually, she'd wondered if one day, he'd simply disappear and never show back up again. Now that felt like a potential reality.

"Because you deserve to know the truth," Plato explained.

"Why now, though?"

"Because the timing is important," Plato stated. "As powerful as I am, I can't save you from everything. Once you set off, I can't follow you."

"But you saved me the last time," Liv argued.

"You were only to that first ridge." Plato indicated the place where Liv had found her mother's sword. "The signal repels me. I nearly couldn't get to you when you fell."

Liv gulped. She knew Plato had weakened himself to save her when she fell from the ridge, but she'd had no idea of the degree of danger for him. "So you won't be following me. Usually, when I don't see you, I still know that you're there. But you won't be once I set off for the top, will you?"

He shook his head. "I can't go up there. I'm sorry."

"Just because my parents told you to watch out for me, it doesn't mean you have to," Liv said, surprised by the sudden bitterness in her voice.

"Liv, yes, I came to you because I was obligated, but I've stayed because I wanted to," Plato repeated. "And your parents didn't ask me to stay beside Ian, who was next in line to be Warrior. They asked me to watch over *you*. I think they knew you'd be one to change everything. They had to have known that one day it would all come down to you."

"Again, why are you telling me this now?" Liv's voice echoed, her emotion cutting her in two.

"Because I need you to know that if things fall apart, if you lose your magic, if you feel like you can't go on," Plato said, real conviction in his voice, "remember with every fiber of your being that I've seen everything in this world. I've been here since the beginning. I'm fueled by magic as old as this Earth. That which created Papa Creola also made me. And Liv, if anything happens to you, I hope that same power quickly takes me from this place."

"Plato," Liv said, her voicing cracking so painfully that it stole her breath.

"Liv Beaufont, watching over you has been the greatest honor of my very long life," Plato continued. "Not being able to follow you into this battle is by far the worst thing that has happened to me, but I have to let you go. I just want you to know how much I sincerely care about you. And I'm not telling you this in case you don't return. I'm telling you this so that you will."

## CHAPTER THIRTY-TWO

Liv was so floored by Plato's confession that she didn't respond right away. By the time she'd found her voice, he'd disappeared, and Stefan stepped through the portal.

He stared around, disoriented. "Something was wrong with the portal."

She nodded. "My best friend did it."

Stefan gave her a questioning look. "Oh, is that person here?"

Liv looked around, a strange peace in her heart. "Yes, for now, he is. And he's not a person. He's the most incredible magical creature in the world."

With a smile, Stefan shook his head. "You are such an enigma. Will I ever know all your secrets?"

"God, I hope not," Liv said with a sigh. "How boring would that be!"

Stefan glanced up at the peak, his eyes shaded by his hand. "So that's our destination. Should we sing on the way up?"

"You can, but I might kill you."

He chuckled. "Okay, so no to singing. I've got a whole pile of knock-knock jokes. How about that?"

Liv reached out and grabbed Stefan's shirt, an expression of mock anger on her face. "How about no?"

He clamped his hand over hers, a sideways grin on his face. "I like you when you pretend you're mad. Well, really, I like you always."

Liv pulled him closer, her mouth inches from his. He leaned in. When he was just about to kiss her, she pushed him to the side, striding past him. "We better get going," she said, hiding the sly grin on her face.

"Oh, you tease," he said, catching up with her easily.

"The hike should take us several hours from here," Liv stated.

"It will take *you* several hours," he bantered back at her. "I'd be up there already if I wasn't waiting for you."

She laughed. "Don't make me change my mind about bringing you with me."

"Oh, I won't," Stefan said. "I'm hoping you'll think it's the best decision you've made. Then you won't want to get rid of me."

"I do like working alone, though," Liv said.

"Yes, but no one is an island."

"And after this, I've got to go back to working for Father Time."

"Who knows what the world will look like after this?" Stefan said.

Liv could hardly fathom that possibility. This was what the Beaufonts had been trying to do from the beginning—reunite mortals with magic. Her parents had made this same hike to disrupt the signal. It was surreal to realize she was following in their actual footsteps.

She glanced sideways at Stefan, grateful that she wasn't alone on this mission. She did like working alone, or so she had thought, but in truth, Liv had never actually been alone. Plato had been there, and now Stefan was. In the future, she'd have others by her side. That was how the best things in this world were done, with the help of friends.

"You're smiling," Stefan said, studying her expression.

"No, I'm not," she argued.

"Then what do you call that look on your face?" he asked.

"Indigestion," she lied.

"You're beautifully ridiculous."

"And you're—"

Stefan halted, throwing his arm in front of Liv protectively.

"What is it?" she asked in a whisper.

He sniffed. "Demons."

"Here?" she questioned, pulling Bellator from its sheath. "Well, looks like I brought the right person with me."

Stefan didn't laugh as she'd expected. His face was pale, a strange expression covering his features. "There's something not right about these demons."

"When is there anything right about a soul-sucking demon?" Liv asked.

He shook his head. "I don't know what's going on yet. I can't figure out what I'm sensing, but be on guard."

"Of course," Liv said, allowing Stefan to take the spot in front of her. Never before had the potential of demons being present worried him. He was immune to their attacks. However, from his stance, he was deathly afraid of what lay ahead.

Liv kept scanning the ground under their feet, remembering when demons had hidden in the dirt so they could pull Stefan down in an attempt to suffocate him. She was so focused on studying the ground that she ran into Stefan when he stopped suddenly.

"Sorry," she said, and quickly shut her mouth when she glanced up. Her chest constricted, and her breath blew between her lips. "It wasn't demons that you were sensing."

"No, something much worse," he said, his arm protectively around her. "Tourists."

## CHAPTER THIRTY-THREE

Adler had expected Olivia Beaufont to come after him. He had bet on it. She was too late, though. Not only was the signal killing mortals all over the world, but it also couldn't be stopped. He'd seen to that. The magic tech powering the signal was too powerful.

Unfortunately, the signal hadn't worked based on proximity, which meant that the mortals climbing the Matterhorn hadn't been affected yet. Adler backed away from the orb that showed him Olivia Beaufont and Stefan Ludwig ascending the peak. He'd set up security to warn him if anyone with magic made the climb. He should have suspected that she'd recruit the demon hunter. Stefan might be good at hunting demons, but how would he do without magic?

He wrote out the message to Talon. The God Magician didn't even have to enter the Chamber of the Tree to lock someone's magic. He was powerful enough that he was connected to multiple areas of the House, one of them being the system that held the magicians' magic.

After sending the message to the God Magician, Adler laughed. Liv wouldn't make it far without magic. Just like her parents and siblings, she'd quickly realize how weak she was without it.

When Talon sent back a confirmation, Adler hurried over to the observation window. The mortals hiking up the peak were mere specks from that distance. However, he didn't need to see them clearly for this spell to work. All he had to do was pull on the dark magic that filled the mountain. It had protected the signal for years, and right now, it would fuel his spell. Adler muttered the incantation that had been one of the first curses. It created monsters out of men.

***

"I don't understand," Liv said as they passed a tour group headed down. "I thought you sensed evil."

"I don't get it either," Stefan said in a hushed voice. "I mean, tourists are pretty annoying, but not necessarily evil."

"Maybe it's Adler." Liv pointed to the summit, where she expected he was guarding the signal. That had been their best guess as to his whereabouts, anyway.

"I'm used to him," Stefan stated. "This is something different. It's like a darkness lurking somewhere, but it's not like anything I've felt before."

"So, not a demon or a vampire or a werewolf?" Liv asked.

He shook his head. "No, I don't sense that it's a thing or person. It feels more like an energy."

"You're getting all metaphysical on me now," Liv joked. "Please tell me you're not turning into a dirty hippie who is going to read my aura."

"Oh, you're not into that?" he teased. "I was hoping we could sip kombucha and review each other's star charts after this whole thing was over."

Liv rolled her eyes. "And we're officially done."

Stefan whipped around, feigning a hurt expression. "Seriously, you're already dumping me? I knew you wouldn't put up with me for long, but I was hoping we'd make it more than a day."

"Fine, I'll give you another chance, but any more hippie bullshit and I'm kicking you to the curb."

"Noted," Stefan said, ambling on. "Any other rules I should be aware of?"

"No cute nicknames."

"Like snugglebutt?" he asked.

"And you're done again."

"No, no, no," he said in a rush. "I was only asking about gross nicknames like snugglebutt."

"Okay, fine. And yes, no cute names that will make me want to puke. Also, don't ever take a picture of me when I'm asleep. Actually, don't watch me when I sleep. That's totally creepy."

"When is this occasion that I'll have to not watch you sleep? Do I wake up in your bed, or do you wake up in mine?" Stefan asked.

"As I was saying," Liv continued, "Bad table manners are a deal breaker."

"Good thing I took that etiquette course."

"If you leave your clothes on the floor, they will go in the trash," Liv stated.

"Again, when is this occasion that I'll have to not leave my clothes on the floor?"

"Never, if you don't watch yourself."

"Did I leave these clothes on the floor after you ripped them off my body?" Stefan teased.

Liv shook her head, suppressing a grin. "Don't grab food off my plate without asking first. Never, ever, sing my name. If you say you're going to do something, then do it. I don't like people who talk but don't follow through. Also, use headphones when you're listening to music on your phone. No one wants to hear your teenie-bop ballads. And most importantly, don't ask me if I've seen a movie and then synopsize it for me."

"I think this is going to go smoothly," Stefan said proudly. "Do you want to know my list of dos and don'ts?"

"Not really," Liv said, picking up her pace and passing Stefan on the path.

"But what if you do something I don't like?" he asked.

"Get over it or dump me," Liv stated, noting another group of hikers who were trotting down the mountain. However, they were moving strangely.

She halted, this time extending her arm to stop Stefan.

He tensed. "What is it?"

She pointed ahead. "Does something appear wrong with those mortals?"

Stefan squinted at the group. His mouth fell open. "No, they can't be."

"I believe they are," she said. "Draw your weapon. It looks like we've got zombies to deal with."

# CHAPTER THIRTY-FOUR

Clark's nerves made him shake as he paged through the *Forbidden Archives*. It didn't seem right that he was sitting in Liv's apartment while she went after the evil man who killed their parents.

However, he knew she was right to leave him behind. They couldn't both go. He wasn't designed for fighting or adventures. He had been born a Councilor through and through.

Like many history books, the *Forgotten Archives* wasn't that interesting. Yes, it had been fascinating at first to learn how the Great War had started between mortals and magicians. One man, a Sinclair, had stood against the Mortal Seven, stating that they had no business weighing in on matters they knew nothing about. From there, things had escalated, until the war couldn't be stopped.

When the magicians won the war, this founder took many steps to force mortals out of the House for good. One was the signal broadcasting from the Matterhorn. Then he sealed the real history in the *Forgotten Archives* and buried it at sea so that it wouldn't be found. But before that, he did something to ensure that he would be incredibly powerful and therefore almost impossible to kill.

"The founders of the House have a unique strength running through their veins," the book had stated. "Therefore, if a member of the House takes the life of another, either a Councilor or a Warrior, they absorb their life force, making them even stronger."

Clark's head whipped up. "That means…"

His eyes darted back to the text, and he scanned the page. There was only one way to combat the power a magician had stolen when murdering another House member. It wasn't complicated, but without it, Liv would be doomed.

She had no idea that Adler would be impossible for her to kill. How could she? But he had murdered their parents and Reese and Ian, which meant he'd absorbed their power and was much stronger than he should be.

Clark jumped up from his place on the sofa, searching for the anywhere pad. He had to warn Liv before it was too late.

## CHAPTER THIRTY-FIVE

Whatever had possessed the mortals approaching Liv and Stefan was dark, evil magic. Once humans, the monsters lumbered forward, their eyes bloodshot and their mouths hanging open in evident hunger. They clawed at each other, gunning for the front position. Their faces were ashen gray, and high-pitched screams spilled from their mouths.

"I think we should try to knock them back," Stefan said, holding up his hand.

Liv expected a blast to shoot from his palm and hit the beasts, giving them an advantage. However, nothing happened.

Stefan looked at his hand like there was something wrong with it. Again he positioned it toward the approaching zombies. Again nothing happened.

"Your magic has been locked," Liv realized at once. She held up her own hand and sent a blast of wind at the zombies. It worked, and this time they flew back several feet, crashing into sharp rocks.

"Well, that's just fine," he said, not at all deterred. "Adler can lock my magic, but that won't stop my demon blood."

In a flash, he disappeared, moving faster than Liv's eyes could process. Instantly, he was on the other side of the ridge, slaughtering zombies with impressive grace. She shook her head and smiled despite herself. There was something to admire about a man who wasn't easily discouraged. Many would have panicked or complained. Not Stefan Ludwig. Seconds after finding out he had no magic, he had sprung straight into battle.

Liv rushed after him. "Don't have all the fun without me."

---

The rattling was the first thing to catch Adler's attention. It was a slight noise, but he knew it wasn't right.

Abandoning his position by the windows, where he had been sending more zombies after Olivia and Stefan, he hurried to the magic tech in the middle of the facility.

A loud buzzing noise radiated from the large machine. Smoke shot up from the wires on the side.

"Oh, hell!" he yelled, pointing his finger at the small fire that had broken out. Nothing happened.

He couldn't understand what could be causing the problem, and there was no reason that he shouldn't have magic. Again he tried to stop the fire, but his magic was too weak to do anything. That didn't make any sense.

Frantically looking around, he found a blanket. Like a revolting mortal, he went to work trying to manually put out the fire. The signal was still broadcasting, but something was definitely wrong with it. Maybe that was what was affecting his magic? he wondered. He'd been able to create the zombies, but that might have been because he was pulling from the dark magic inside the Matterhorn.

Closing his eyes, Adler drew that power into him. Then he pointed his finger at the magic tech. Instantly the humming stopped, the fire went out, and the signal strengthened.

Adler flexed his fingers, seeing the blackness start in his fingertips and spread up his hands through his veins. He'd allowed dark magic into his system. There was no way of ridding himself of it now, but that was fine. That was how Talon had come so far, and Adler was ready to join him and lead the House of Seven.

## CHAPTER THIRTY-SIX

Fighting zombies was about like slaughtering demons, except that demons were dumber and stronger. So there were pros and cons, Liv realized, pulling the sword from a zombie's stomach and swinging it around to lop off the head off another one.

Although Stefan had killed quite a few, by the time she showed up, the number of zombies had doubled. They just kept coming.

With her back up against Stefan's, Liv surveyed the area. "Any bright ideas about how we get rid of these guys?"

"I have a few, actually," he said, launching himself forward and thrusting his sword into one zombie's chest while side-kicking another one, sending him down the side of the steep slope.

Liv took this opportunity to shoot a few fireballs at three approaching zombies. Adler had to have turned every mortal on the mountain into the walking dead. Liv instantly felt remorse for the mortals who were innocent in this but victims of this war. All she could do was get past them and hope to save the rest of humanity.

"So, these ideas," Liv said, throwing a fireball over her shoulder and knocking out a zombie that was about to pounce on Stefan.

He glanced over his shoulder with surprise. "Hey, thanks."

"No problem," she said, catching her breath as the next wave of zombies approached.

"I think you need to go that way," he said, pointing to where the path split.

"Why?" Liv asked, sending out more fireballs to halt the progress of the monsters. "The summit is to the right."

"And I'm guessing that wherever this magic tech is, it won't be on the beaten path," Stefan explained.

"Good point," Liv stated. "Actually, I should have considered that it's entirely hidden. There's got to be a way to reveal it."

"I'm sure you can use your magic to figure it out," Stefan said, wiping his blade clean and preparing for the next wave of zombies. "Must be nice."

Liv winked at him. "We'll get your magic back."

"Don't worry about me," he said confidently. "I'll be fine. But you can't stay here fighting zombies—"

"But—"

"Liv, you have to get up there and stop the signal," Stefan cut in. "Mortals are in danger, and that means magic is too. Me not having magic isn't that big of a deal if everyone doesn't have it."

"But I can't leave you here."

"Of course, you can," he stated. "I'll hold off the zombies. You get past them and go after Adler. I'll be fine."

Liv knew he was right, but she didn't want to admit it. Finally, she nodded reluctantly. "Fine, but let me at least help you with this next group."

"Go now," he encouraged. "And no more fireballs. We don't know how much longer you'll have magic. I'll be fine."

Liv didn't want to leave him, but she knew she had to. She gave Stefan one last look before sprinting up the path that led away from the summit.

---

Clark frantically scribbled on the anywhere pad.

*Liv, are you there?*

A moment later a response scrolled across the blank page.

*I'm sort of busy right now.*

Clark quickly wrote a reply. *This is important.*

*More important than not getting eaten by zombies?* Liv asked.

Even in battle, she's making jokes, Clark thought, shaking his head. *Yes, but don't get eaten by zombies.*

*What is it, bro?*

He let out a breath. *It's about Adler. He's more powerful than we thought.*

A moment later, Liv's words appeared. *Hence the freaking zombies.*

Clark nodded. *Yes, but that's not all. You can't simply kill him since he absorbed our family's lives when they died, making him stronger.*

*Oh, shit.*

Quickly Clark referenced the *Forgotten Archives*, ensuring he got the information correct. *There's an easy way to combat it, though.*

*I'm listening,* Liv replied.

*You're not going to like it.*

Clark could almost hear the eye roll from on the other side of the world.

*I suspected as much,* Liv wrote. *What do I have to do?*

*You can't kill him with magic,* Clark explained.

*I figured you'd say something ridiculous like that,* Liv fired back.

He almost wanted to laugh. She was doing an impressive job of replying, considering she was in battle.

*Liv, you have to spill your own blood.*

*Oh, dude, that's so gross,* Liv shot back.

*And then you have to kill Adler with your own hands.*

There wasn't a response for a long moment. When it finally came through, Clark's chest lightened slightly.

*I was already planning on doing that.*

## CHAPTER THIRTY-SEVEN

Liv slid the anywhere pad back into her cape. She was grateful she didn't mind the sight of blood. Her experience fighting demons and other bad guys had gotten her over that pretty fast. However, she still didn't like the sight of her own blood. Still, whatever it took to rid the world of the last Sinclair would be worth it. She daydreamed of a time in the future when the Sinclair family would be replaced in the House. Another magical family would come in, one that wasn't corrupt down to their very core as well as power-hungry.

Often Liv checked over her shoulder, spying on Stefan's battle with the zombies below. She'd hiked such a far distance that it was hard to make out the details, but he was still standing, and that was what counted most. She consoled herself with the fact that the demon blood should heal him if he was bitten by a zombie. It was incredibly helpful stuff if one didn't mind nearly dying to have the blood running through their veins.

That strange wind from before ran across Liv's cheeks,

sending her back a step. She halted, sensing that things weren't what they seemed. Holding up her hand, she tried to clear the space ahead of her. She needed to see what was actually there and not the glamour that covered it. However, she didn't have magic. She knew at her core that it hadn't been locked. That would have been impossible. Like a faucet being turned on, she could feel magic trickling through her. There just wasn't much of it.

This was Adler's doing. He was killing mortals and taking the magic from this world. She had to stop him.

Closing her eyes, Liv focused on the one thing she knew was the purest form of her magic. It was the only thing that could restore her magic if every mortal died. This source was timeless. It was all-encompassing. It was infinite.

It was the love she had for her family.

With her eyes closed, Liv repeated the words her mother had taught her. The ones that were more powerful than any spell in the world: "*Familia est sempiternum.*"

There were few things as incredible in the world as Liv Beaufont. Stefan would happily face down a thousand zombies without magic for that woman. However, he might have gotten a bit in over his head with these particular monsters. They kept coming, crawling over the sides of the cliffs and scurrying out of caves. He had no idea where they were coming from. Adler had to have resurrected every dead and living person on this mountain.

When the forces were almost overwhelming him,

Stefan drew them down the mountain, trying to pull them away from where Liv had gone. He didn't see any zombies on the path she'd taken. They were coming after him, and he had to keep it that way.

He pulled out his other sword, slicing zombie after zombie. However, there were always more ready to attack him.

Thrown off balance when a zombie took out his legs, Stefan tumbled several hundred yards down the slope, rolling end over end. The fall would have killed him if it hadn't been for his demon blood. He looked at a deep cut on his forearm as he tried to stand. It sealed up almost immediately. He pulled his swords from where they'd stuck in the dirt and glanced up. A solid wall of zombies was approaching. It didn't matter that Stefan had demon blood. He was hard to kill, but not impossible. Several hundred zombies were all it would take.

He pressed his fingers to his lips and kissed them. "Liv, I hope you make it. And I hope you know how amazing I always thought you were."

Stefan brought his swords up, ready to go out with a bang. But something flickered at the corner of his vision, catching his attention.

Standing beside him as casually as if waiting for a bus was a black and white cat.

"Ummm, are you lost?" Stefan asked the feline.

The animal looked at him with a sly grin. "No, but I think you could use some help, unless you'd like to meet an untimely death."

"I wouldn't, actually," Stefan stated. "Do you know of anyone who can help."

"I do," the cat said. "Thankfully, you rolled into a territory where I can be of assistance."

"And who are you?" Stefan asked, realizing he was talking to an animal.

"I'm Liv's best friend, and you're someone she won't want to die. Which are the only reasons I'm talking to you now."

*A cat? I've got a cat to help me with a hundred zombies?* Stefan thought defeatedly. He shrugged it off, trying to focus.

Stefan nodded, preparing for the first wave of zombies. "Well, okay, kitty. Show me what you got."

## CHAPTER THIRTY-EIGHT

Liv knew instantly that her magic had returned. She could feel it flowing in her veins like her family's blood. It was one and the same.

She also knew that her magic was back because on the hill above her, out of nowhere, a large building had materialized. From it, she could plainly see a beam of red light broadcasting out to the world.

With a deep breath, she took a step. It was time to finally end this.

———

Liv had the best friends, Stefan thought as he cleanly sliced off a zombie's head. In a swift movement, he swung around, slashing at three more zombies and sending them back several feet.

He had doubted the little kitty would be much help. Man, had he been wrong. When he wasn't looking, the animal had transformed into a large black panther and was currently mowing down zombies, killing them faster than he was. In a matter of minutes, he and his new friend had made short work of the zombies.

Stefan looked proudly up at the summit, where he hoped Liv was currently. Maybe today wasn't his last day on this Earth. He would happily slaughter a thousand zombies if it meant he could continue to fight beside Liv Beaufont.

There was no one in the world like her.

He caught a glimpse as the giant panther ran over a zombie, sliced another with a bat of his paw, and sank his teeth into a third.

"Liv has the absolute coolest friends," Stefan stated, impressed.

***

The door to the facility wasn't locked, which seemed like a no-brainer to Liv. She pushed it open and immediately sucked in a breath. The fumes wafting from the magic tech in the middle of the room burned her lungs. A hot wind circulated through the space, crisping her face. And standing in the middle of the room was the man she'd come to kill.

## CHAPTER THIRTY-NINE

Adler Sinclair's long white hair fell down his narrow back. He had his hands extended beside him and chin tilted upward as he marveled at the red beam that shot straight through the opening in the roof and out into the world. It was the signal that kept mortals from seeing magic. It was what was killing them.

Liv held up her hand, but almost instantly, she was lifted into the air by an invisible force and thrown back down to the floor. Her head hit the stone hard, making her taste blood.

The figure who seemed taller than Adler turned around. It was in fact the man she'd grown to hate, but he was different. More powerful. The veins in his face were black, especially around his pale eyes, which were glowing red.

All Liv could think was that he was polluted somehow, but all the wondering in the world wasn't worth her time or attention. She had more pressing matters.

"So you got past the zombies, did you?" Adler asked, striding forward, the hot wind rushing past his robes.

"What zombies?" Liv asked, scrambling to her feet.

He grimaced at her. "You've been a pain in my side from the beginning. I regretted what happened to your parents and your siblings, but I'll enjoy what I do to you."

"You mean when you murdered them?" Liv yelled, her fury unleashed for the first time ever.

With a flick of his wrist, Liv was sent flying into the opposite stone wall. Her jaw smacked against it, and she slid down in a heap of disillusionment to the floor.

"Oh, your smart mouth has always been your shortcoming," Adler stated.

Liv slid her hand across her mouth, wiping away the blood. Undeterred, she pushed back up. "Why do you hate mortals? Why do you want them gone?"

The question, as Liv had intended, made Adler pause. He was all ego, and therefore, he would need to explain his case. Legitimatize it.

"We never needed them," he said smugly. "They are waste. Originally they were supposed to be slaves for the magical races. However, they rose up and took positions in the House, and then they went too far."

"They shouldn't be our slaves," Liv ground out through clenched teeth.

Adler laughed, no humor in his tone. "You think you know so much. Always trying to upstage me in front of the council. Your punishment will be long and painful."

Liv was unsurprised when her feet lifted off the floor and she flew at the window on the far side of the room. Thankfully, she didn't fly through it, but she cracked it severely with her spine. When she fell to the ground, the glass shattered, raining down on her. Liv covered her face and rolled over on her stomach.

Because there were obviously no time-outs, Adler picked Liv up by the back of the neck and hauled her to her feet. "I've worked way too hard for you to ruin things. The Beaufonts seem to think it is their right to expose the truth, but soon it won't matter. Soon mortals will all be dead, and magic will reign."

Doing the thing only thing available to her, Liv kicked her feet wildly, knocking Adler straight in the shin. He yelped in pain and dropped her as he reached for his lower leg.

Liv scrambled away, running past the source of the signal and surveying it quickly. The power source was thankfully on the ground. All she had to do was get close enough.

Like a wind blowing across the floor, Adler arrived in front of her in an instant, regarding her with those blood-red eyes. "I'll enjoy killing you. It will only add to my power."

"The thing is," Liv told him, peering around him, "I wasn't really planning on dying yet. And about that power that you've stolen? I'm here to take it back."

Adler, who never liked her jokes, actually laughed. Then he lifted his hand, which was covered in black veins. But Liv was already prepared. She raised her palm into the air, blocking the spell he'd shot at her. She couldn't use magic to kill him, but she could use it to defend herself.

Continuous lightning shot between Adler and Liv's hand, bouncing back and forth as she tried to keep him back. He was incredibly powerful, a force unlike any she'd ever encountered, but still, she was able to push him back several feet. When he was almost to the far wall, she ducked behind the magic tech, swiftly putting the device John had given her into the power source and starting the virus.

Before he could locate her, Liv rolled out from behind the device, pulling Bellator from its sheath.

If Adler was intimidated, he was hiding it. He casually looked at her sword and scoffed. "Do you really think your little sword can kill me?"

Liv shook her head. "No, my giant-made sword can't."

His eyes narrowed. "What are you doing with a giant-made sword?"

"I'm using it to take you down." She turned Bellator around and sliced the blade across the palm of her hand. Her blood dripped from her palm to the floor, landing strangely like plumes of smoke.

This obviously threw Adler off, making him frown. "What is this magic?"

Liv stepped forward, dropping Bellator with a loud clang. "It isn't magic, Mr. Sinclair."

He backed up several feet, fear evident in each of his steps. He was confused, and for a man who needed to know what was going on, this was the best possible way to knock him off-balance. With each step, he seemed to shrink, his eyes dulling in appearance.

Liv allowed her blood to drop to the ground, sending smoke up. She pressed her fingers into her palm, making the blood leak out faster. With each drop, the strength drained out of the man before her.

"My blood is the same as that which ran through Guinevere Beaufont's veins. And you killed her, taking my mother from this world," Liv said, tears aching in her throat.

Adler stumbled back over wires, falling on his backside.

"Theodore Beaufont was the best man I've ever known, and you killed him because of your selfishness," Liv continued, her blood continuing to spill, leaving a trail behind her.

Adler's skin had returned to its usual appearance, transparent and thin. He shook his head. "No! No!" He raised his hand, but nothing happened.

"My sister Reese was a creative soul who would have gone on to do amazing things, but you couldn't allow that, could you, Mr. Sinclair?"

The smoke from Liv's blood wrapped around her like a cape, making her feel powerful. Supported. Loved.

Adler had backed up to the far wall. His hair was falling out suddenly, and his face was covered in wrinkles. Whatever magic was at work here wasn't normal. It was the undoing of evil.

"And Ian," Liv began. "He was braver than you or Decar or any other Warrior out there."

"Decar…" Adler said, his eyes lighting up.

"Yes, if your brother was alive, you could summon him, drawing on his strength, exactly as I'm pulling my family's power from you." Liv tilted her head to the side and opened her bloody palm. "But he's dead. My giant friends killed him, and we took back the real history."

"No!" Adler yelled, but it was too late.

Liv lifted him into the air using magic, the same way

he'd done to her. However, when he was high enough, she released the magic binding him, gifted to her by her family's blood. Liv wrapped her hands about Adler Sinclair's throat and pressed, cutting off his supply of oxygen. His weak attempts to fight her were futile. Liv was an incredibly strong Warrior for the House of Fourteen. Every mission he'd sent her on to endanger her life had prepared her for this moment, making her stronger than the weak man before her.

After only a short moment, Adler's body went limp. It wasn't the grand ending she'd pictured, but it worked. Liv stepped back, allowing Adler to fall lifeless to the ground, his neck covered in her blood. And then it turned to smoke, igniting him and turning him into a bonfire.

Liv jumped back, fanning away the smoke.

She glanced over her shoulder at the magic tech. The huge beam of light was gone. The device had worked. The signal was dead.

The fire fueled by Adler's body was growing. Liv picked up Bellator and ran for the door. She was only a few yards from the facility when an explosion threw her forward. She rolled, covering her head. When she turned back, she was certain of one important thing.

That piece of magical tech would never operate again.

## CHAPTER FORTY

The council was silent for a long moment. Finally, Haro looked up, pure amazement on his face.

"Everything you say here is true?"

Liv caught Stefan staring at her before she nodded. "Yes, it's all true. Soon mortals will be recovering from the attempt to murder them. Then they will see magic for the first time in over a century."

Clark held up the *Forgotten Archives*. "I've made copies of this book and sent it to each of you. It will fill in everything you need to know."

Raina shook her head. "This is so…strange. House of Fourteen? Why didn't we know that?"

"Adler Sinclair had been working on this for a long time," Liv explained. "He murdered my family. He did everything he could to keep the truth buried."

"But why?" Hester asked.

Liv lifted her chin, calling on the strength she'd felt on the top of the Matterhorn. "Because he was afraid that mortals would change magic, but what we need to know is that magic only exists because of mortals. They are the moral compass we need in this House to regulate our power."

"Is this about registering magic?" Lorenzo asked.

"No," Clark cut in. "That's the opposite of what we need. That's control, which solves nothing except to turn power over to those who aren't qualified. Instead, we need to come together. That starts with mortals coming into the House. And then elves, gnomes, giants, and whoever else will help us to maintain justice."

"You can't really be insinuating that we should allow other magical races as well as mortals into this place?" Bianca asked, her tone high-pitched.

Liv cut her eyes at Emilio. "I'm absolutely suggesting that. And we need to stop worrying about diluting our bloodlines and instead concern ourselves with loving one another."

"This will take time," Haro said cautiously.

"Then it will," Liv stated with authority. "But it will start today."

"Who are you to tell us what will start today or anything else?!" Bianca screamed.

Liv held out her hand casually, and a holographic image of Father Time appeared. "I've decreed that Liv Beaufont, Warrior for the House of Fourteen, will be in charge of rounding up the Mortal Seven and returning them to their rightful spots. Once they are in place, I expect the House to serve justice as it was always intended to do. Anyone who opposes my order will see their time on Earth cut dramatically short. If you have any questions, concerns, or suggestions, please see my elf delegates."

Liv closed her palm when Papa Creola's speech was over. "Well, I say you argue with Father Time on this one, Bianca. Really tell him off. I'll give you his direct line."

"This is ridiculous!" Bianca yelled, rising to her feet and running from the Chamber of the Tree.

Liv shook her head, hiding the grin that was begging to be released.

Haro leaned forward. "This is a lot for the Council to digest. However, there's no way to refute the evidence you've presented. Warrior Beaufont, you have your orders. Other Warriors, your jobs are to help mortals acclimate to the changes about to befall them.

"The rest of us will need to brush up on the forgotten history, and then I suggest we all come together. There has been a lot of treachery among our members, but I hope we can put it behind us to create a better tomorrow for mortals and the magical races."

"To a better tomorrow," Hester said, and the others in the room repeated her words, tightening Liv's chest and making her realize that happy endings might actually be possible.

## CHAPTER FORTY-ONE

The bones crunched under Talon's foot as he tried to take a step forward. He crumpled to the ground again. The opening to the Black Void was far away, and he was still so weak. Yes, he could control things in the House from this place, but he couldn't influence them the way he needed to.

Decar was gone.

Adler was dead.

He was all the Sinclairs had left.

And he was going to have to get stronger faster if he was going to stop this.

Talon had won this war once, and he would do it again. One girl might have brought mortals back, but it wouldn't last. All he had to do was wait, recuperate, and draw on magical reserves, and one day, he'd be strong enough to rise again.

In the meantime, he'd have to wake someone to help him.

Lying his face on the cold stone floor, he searched in his

mind for the girl he was connected to through blood, Adler's deceased sister's child—an orphan who had gone unnoticed. However, she was a Sinclair, and she was powerful. Only a young girl, but an illusionist, and the rightful person to inherit the role as Sinclair Warrior for the House of Seven. He would need her to move forward, to take over what was rightfully his.

Talon drew her to him with a power no Sinclair could resist.

Across the globe, Kayla Sinclair awoke suddenly, sweat beading her forehead. She'd had the strangest dream. But it wasn't a dream.

She pushed her blankets off her lap and stood suddenly, her long white hair falling over her shoulders. Although she wasn't sure why, she knew she needed to get to Los Angeles immediately. She was needed at the House of Seven. There was a role that needed to be filled, and it was her birthright.

CHAPTER FORTY-TWO

"Well, that was easy," Stefan said, when the last Councilor filed out of the Chamber of the Tree. For once, Liv had stayed behind after the meeting, telling them she needed some time there to think. Stefan had stayed too, and now they were face to face, with the lights of the tree twinkling over their heads.

"Yeah, we just had to battle a few hundred zombies, kill a madman, and wake up the entire population of mortals," Liv said casually.

"I didn't even break a sweat," he said with a wink.

From the corner of her vision, Liv saw Jude stride out of the darkness. She tensed.

"What is it?" Stefan asked, sensing her stress.

"Oh, nothing. It's just that Jude and I are working through some trust issues," Liv said as Diabolos landed beside the white tiger. She relaxed.

Stefan pointed to the other side of the room, where two green eyes shone in the dark. "I think you're safe as long as your best friend is around."

Surprised that Plato was showing himself in front of another, Liv nodded. "Yeah, I'm really lucky. I have the best people in my life."

"I think we're the lucky ones," Stefan said, reaching out and grabbing Liv's cape. He tugged her forward, and she allowed it.

Out of everything that had happened, this was the most surprising part. Liv had expected to avenge her parents' death. There was never a reality where she didn't fight to the death to finish what they had started, and she was not going to stop until mortals were freed from the brainwashing. But love? That hadn't been in the cards. Or at least, she hadn't expected it.

Stefan cupped Liv's chin, gazing into her eyes with quiet reverence. She couldn't think of a better happy ending, and yet, she knew that matters were far from over. There was still so much left to do, restore and fix.

So, as the demon hunter laid his lips on hers, she settled for a "happy right now." Tomorrow would bring its own challenges and adventures, and she'd be ready to face them with her team by her side.

I'm currently on a flight to New Orleans as I write these notes. I'm going back home after almost eight years to visit my family. I requested that my parents take Lydia and I on a swamp tour. I'm certain that this is going to lead to some awesome inspiration for the next book. I expect a fight scene in the swamps and French Quarter and a whole lot of puns about Liv feeling "swamped."

So Adler is gone, but a new villain is rising up to take his place. And the God Magician… I'm excited for the third arc of this book. It's amazing how much everyone has progressed. And some of the reveals in this installment actually surprised me. I didn't see the reunion with Liv's mother coming or the secret regarding the Beaufonts.

And Plato. Damn it. That cat sort of, kind of made me tear up. He's got some secret and I'll be damned if I don't even know what it is. I've written 49 books and the very best reveals, I never saw coming. And they totally made sense when I looked back. That happened with the Black Void in this series. I was compelled to put it in in the first book. A fellow writer who I told about it said, "Oh, it should be this…" I was like, "No, I know it's not going to be that, but I'm not sure what it's supposed to be." I have that a lot when writing, although I'm most certainly not a panster. I loosely plot every book. However, I always leave room for a little bit of spontaneous creative freedom.

It was like book five when the God Magician was introduced. You can correct me if I'm wrong on that. I can't recall entirely. Anyway, I had that beautiful ah-ha moment when I realized what the Black Void was supposed to be. It was always where the God Magician was hiding, but I didn't know it, which meant it makes it even better for you the reader, or at least I hope it does. And I'm hoping it will also be the same with Plato's secret. I also didn't know that Plato had that deal with Liv's parents until this book and I was shocked. That's how creativity works.

I spoke to someone recently who wondered if I was a tortured writer who was told by my characters to write their story. "Sometimes" is the answer. But also, I like to think that I'm a channel, a storyteller, if you will, who has been assigned to tell the stories of people who I don't know. Maybe they are in another dimension or realm or whatever. And for whatever reason, I have access to the channel that broadcasts their stories. Anyway, that probably makes me sound nuts. But so does the confession that I hear voices, which I do.

And then there's the thing with Stefan. I totally saw that coming. I've been looking forward to it actually. Some of you readers have been asking for the romance. I hope this was what you wanted and when you wanted it. Romance is tricky like that. It needs to come at the right time and when we are ready for it. That's true for us in the literary sense and literally as well.

However, to be honest, writing romance isn't really my thing anymore. I used to write YA love triangle stuff. Since then I've gotten away from it. Thank the gods. But I realize how much I've missed that romantic tension in a story. I was telling Lydia the other day that every good story has romance. She, of course, grimaced at me and pretended to vomit.

It only took me eight books to introduce some romance. I knew that Stefan and Liv were going to get together at some point, but it needed to make sense. Liv needed to be in the right place. And something that I learned, I did too.

Now, who can resist a tall, dark and handsome demon hunter? Not me. If someone has a friend, brother, cousin who meets Stefan's description then sign me up. I'm almost certain I can't find someone like that on the dating app, not that I'm swiping.

In all seriousness, I ended a relationship with a guy a few days before I finished this book. I knew that I'd be writing these more romantic scenes and worried how my relationship status would affect my creativity. Yes, that's how my practical brain works. I worry how my personal life will affect my brain for writing. Maybe my priorities are out of whack. I can almost guarantee that they are.

Anyway, don't tell anyone (I know you won't because you're good like that and we're friends), but I worried how doing this break up would affect this book. Would I go through a funk? Would I be in processing mode? Would I slack because I was consumed with guilt or concern or whatever emotions people with a heart have?

Well, it turns out that it all worked out, both the break up and the book. I wasn't really feeling the romance with Stefan before this book. And then, bam! I found myself totally crushing on the boy as I wrote about him and Liv at the wedding and then on the Matterhorn. Apparently when I cut the real boy out of my life, I made room for a fictional boyfriend. I'm actually completely fine with this. Book boyfriends don't leave their clothes on the floor, chew with their mouth open and sing badly (thereby ruining my favorite song). Well, maybe book boyfriends do that kind of stuff, but I can just shut the book and poof, they're gone.

Michael tends to be entertained by my dating antics, hence why he had me write a book about them. However, I'm going to be the most boring single gal for a while. That way I can focus on Stefan and Liv and the next arc in the series. I love my characters. They are my best friends (don't tell my real friends that).

As I head back from New Orleans (finishing Author Notes now), I'm looking forward to getting back and spending the next week locking myself in my house and writing. Lydia is going with her father on vacation. Poor girl has to go on back to back trips, but she seems excited about it. She travels as much as MA. However, I get to lock myself away and write. Some might think that's lonely business, but not for me. I'm all too happy to hang out alone and work. That's the beauty of loving what you do. And you all make it all the better. Thanks for supporting the books and being completely awesome!

# MICHAEL'S AUTHOR NOTES

## JUNE 13, 2019

THANK YOU for not only reading this story but these Author Notes as well.

(I think I've been good with always opening with "thank you." If not, I need to edit the other Author Notes!)

## RANDOM (sometimes) THOUGHTS?

I wish I could do some kick-ass photoshop work. If I could, I might find that swiper-be-swiping app that Sarah's not using (uh huh) and photoshop some dark, tall, demon-hunter-type guys and provide her with proof she isn't swiping fast enough.

Not that I would play a practical joke on Sarah or anything…

(Oh yes, yes I would.)

Sarah is the quintessential author. She likes to be left alone to write, her best friends all talk to her in her head…

And she says the wrong things at the right time. That comes from staying alone all of the time talking to people in her head.

See how that comes back full circle?

Sarah is one of those people I want to be one day when I grow up. An opinionated (but fun) person who expresses her opinion and doesn't care (for the most part) what happens.

Me? I worry too much.

Except when I speak about Sarah …. (Actually, that's not true. A few books ago she talked about my infamous foot-in-mouth moment talking about how not-tall she is - classic moment of 'DOH!')

If you want to know what Sarah is like, just read the <u>Everyone in LA is an REDACTED</u> books… Or hell, Sarah is Liv, except her cat isn't really as cool.


## AROUND THE WORLD IN 80 DAYS

One of the interesting (at least to me) aspects of my life is the ability to work from anywhere and at any time. In the future, I hope to re-read my own Author Notes and remember my life as a diary entry.

**Las Vegas, Nv Cave in the Sky (™) USA**

I'm setting up my XBOX. Actually, this is my first XBOX in many years. I've been working non-stop (practically) for 3 1/2 years, and now I'm ready to have something that will help me…uh… 'work on my imagination.'

Which, sadly, isn't too far from the truth.

My mom wondered (to my brother, then finally admitted it to me) back when I was writing The Kurtherian Gambit about book 12 or so what would happen when I run out of ideas?

I laughed, telling her that wouldn't be a problem.

Hundreds of stories later, it's a bit of a problem.

Stephen King in his book On Writing mentions taking time to read other stories and working to fill the well of creativity.

He's right.

I've done all sorts of things to rejuvenate my creativity.

It just so happens that this months effort is an XBOX.

Sure hope I didn't choose the wrong game system (meaning I might have needed to get a PS4.)

We shall see.

## FAN PRICING

$0.99 Saturdays (new LMBPN stuff) and $0.99 Wednesday (both LMBPN books and friends of LMBPN books.) Get great stuff from us and others at tantalizing prices.

Go ahead. I bet you can't read just one.

Sign up here: http://lmbpn.com/email/.

## HOW TO MARKET FOR BOOKS YOU LOVE

Review them so others have your thoughts, and tell friends and the dogs of your enemies (because who wants to talk to enemies?)… Enough said ;-)

Ad Aeternitatem,

Michael Anderle

# ACKNOWLEDGMENTS

## SARAH NOFFKE

My favorite part of writing any book is creating the acknowledgements page. It reminds me that writing a book is not a solo task. I might sit alone and write, but the finished product is a result of the support and encouragement of a tribe of people.

Thank you to the readers who buy the books, read them, review and recommend. YOU are the one who keeps us writing. I'm always inspired by the messages I receive from readers. Thank you supporting the books and offering so much richness to my life.

Thank you to my LBMPN family for all the support. Steve, Michael, Lynne, Moonchild, Jennifer and so many others who help champion the book to publication and beyond.

Thank you to the beta readers who offered so many valuable insights early on. Thank you to John, Chrisa, Kelly, Martin and Larry.

Thank you to the JIT team for all the awesome feedback. A new series is always exciting and nerve-wracking.

Michael and I thought we had a great idea for a new world, but we don't really know until we get objective feedback. What would I do without all you awesome readers?

Thank you to my friends and family. Writing is a strange profession. I work weird hours, talk to myself, have a strange diet, get antsy about deadlines. But the wonderful people in my life continue to show their encouragement and thoughtfulness no matter what. It is never lost on me because I know that I wouldn't be doing what I love without all you amazing people, cheering me on.

And as with all my books, the final thank you goes to my muse, Lydia. I wrote my first book so that I could make my daughter proud, and it's never stopped. I write every book for you, my love.

Sarah Noffke writes YA and NA science fiction, fantasy, paranormal and urban fantasy. In addition to being an author, she is a mother, podcaster and professor. Noffke holds a Masters of Management and teaches college business/writing courses. Most of her students have no idea that she toils away her hours crafting fictional characters. www.sarahnoffke.com

**Check out other work by Sarah author here.**

***Ghost Squadron:***

Formation #1:

**Kill the bad guys. Save the Galaxy. All in a hard day's work.**

After ten years of wandering the outer rim of the galaxy, Eddie Teach is a man without a purpose. He was one of the toughest pilots in the Federation, but now he's just a regular guy, getting into bar fights and making a difference wherever he can. It's not the same as flying a ship and saving colonies, but it'll have to do.

That is, until General Lance Reynolds tracks Eddie down and offers him a job. There are bad people out there, plotting terrible things, killing innocent people, and destroying entire colonies. **Someone has to stop them.**

Eddie, along with the genetically-enhanced combat pilot Julianna Fregin and her trusty E.I. named Pip, must recruit a diverse team of specialists, both human and alien. They'll need to master their new Q-Ship, one of the most powerful strike ships ever constructed. And finally, they'll have to stop a faceless enemy so powerful, it threatens to destroy the entire Federation.

**All in a day's work, right?**

Experience this exciting military sci-fi saga and the latest addition to the expanded Kurtherian Gambit Universe. If you're a fan of Mass Effect, Firefly, or Star Wars, you'll love this riveting new space opera.

*NOTE: If cursing is a problem, then this might not be for you.*

*Check out the entire series* here.


*The Precious Galaxy Series:*


*Corruption #1*

**A new evil lurks in the darkness.**

After an explosion, the crew of a battlecruiser mysteriously disappears.

Bailey and Lewis, complete strangers, find themselves

suddenly onboard the damaged ship. Lewis hasn't worked a case in years, not since the final one broke his spirit and his bank account. The last thing Bailey remembers is preparing to take down a fugitive on Onyx Station.

**Mysteries are harder to solve when there's no evidence left behind.**

Bailey and Lewis don't know how they got onboard *Ricky Bobby* or why. However, they quickly learn that whatever was responsible for the explosion and disappearance of the crew is still on the ship.

**Monsters are real and what this one can do changes everything.**

The new team bands together to discover what happened and how to fight the monster lurking in the bottom of the battlecruiser.

**Will they find the missing crew? Or will the monster end them all?**

*The Soul Stone Mage Series:*

House of Enchanted #1:

**The Kingdom of Virgo has lived in peace for thousands of years...until now.**

The humans from Terran have always been real assholes to the witches of Virgo. Now a silent war is brewing, and the timing couldn't be worse. Princess Azure will soon be crowned queen of the Kingdom of Virgo.

**In the Dark Forest a powerful potion-maker has been murdered.**

Charmsgood was the only wizard who could stop a

deadly virus plaguing Virgo. He also knew about the devastation the people from Terran had done to the forest.

**Azure must protect her people. Mend the Dark Forest. Create alliances with savage beasts. No biggie, right?**

*But on coronation day everything changes. Princess Azure isn't who she thought she was and that's a big freaking problem.*

**Welcome to The Revelations of Oriceran. Check out the entire series** here.

### *The Lucidites Series:*

Awoken, #1:
Around the world humans are hallucinating after sleepless nights.

In a sterile, underground institute the forecasters keep reporting the same events.

And in the backwoods of Texas, a sixteen-year-old girl is about to be caught up in a fierce, ethereal battle.

Meet Roya Stark. She drowns every night in her dreams, spends her hours reading classic literature to avoid her family's ridicule, and is prone to premonitions—which are becoming more frequent. And now her dreams are filled with strangers offering to reveal what she has always wanted to know: Who is she? That's the question that haunts her, and she's about to find out. But will Roya live to regret learning the truth?

Stunned, #2
Revived, #3

### *The Reverians Series:*

*Defects*, #1:

In the happy, clean community of Austin Valley, everything appears to be perfect. Seventeen-year-old Em Fuller, however, fears something is askew. Em is one of the new generation of Dream Travelers. For some reason, the gods have not seen fit to gift all of them with their expected special abilities. Em is a Defect—one of the unfortunate Dream Travelers not gifted with a psychic power. Desperate to do whatever it takes to earn her gift, she endures painful daily injections along with commands from her overbearing, loveless father. One of the few bright spots in her life is the return of a friend she had thought dead—but with his return comes the knowledge of a shocking, unforgivable truth. The society Em thought was protecting her has actually been betraying her, but she has no idea how to break away from its authority without hurting everyone she loves.

*Rebels*, #2

*Warriors*, #3

**Vagabond Circus Series:**

*Suspended*, #1:

When a stranger joins the cast of Vagabond Circus—a circus that is run by Dream Travelers and features real magic—mysterious events start happening. The once orderly grounds of the circus become riddled with hidden threats. And the ringmaster realizes not only are his circus and its magic at risk, but also his very life.

Vagabond Circus caters to the skeptics. Without skeptics, it would close its doors. This is because Vagabond

Circus runs for two reasons and only two reasons: first and foremost to provide the lost and lonely Dream Travelers a place to be illustrious. And secondly, to show the nonbelievers that there's still magic in the world. If they believe, then they care, and if they care, then they don't destroy. They stop the small abuse that day-by-day breaks down humanity's spirit. If Vagabond Circus makes one skeptic believe in magic, then they halt the cycle, just a little bit. They allow a little more love into this world. That's Dr. Dave Raydon's mission. And that's why this ringmaster recruits. That's why he directs. That's why he puts on a show that makes people question their beliefs. He wants the world to believe in magic once again.

*Paralyzed, #2*
*Released, #3*

### Ren Series:

Ren: The Man Behind the Monster, #1:
Born with the power to control minds, hypnotize others, and read thoughts, Ren Lewis, is certain of one thing: God made a mistake. No one should be born with so much power. A monster awoke in him the same year he received his gifts. At ten years old. A prepubescent boy with the ability to control others might merely abuse his powers, but Ren allowed it to corrupt him. And since he can have and do anything he wants, Ren should be happy. However, his journey teaches him that harboring so much power doesn't bring happiness, it steals it. Once this realization sets in, Ren makes up his mind to do the one thing

that can bring his tortured soul some peace. He must kill the monster.

*Note* This book is NA and has strong language, violence and sexual references.

*Ren: God's Little Monster, #2*
*Ren: The Monster Inside the Monster, #3*
*Ren: The Monster's Adventure, #3.5*
*Ren: The Monster's Death*

**Olento Research Series:**

*Alpha Wolf, #1:*
Twelve men went missing.

Six months later they awake from drug-induced stupors to find themselves locked in a lab.

And on the night of a new moon, eleven of those men, possessed by new—and inhuman—powers, break out of their prison and race through the streets of Los Angeles until they disappear one by one into the night.

Olento Research wants its experiments back. Its CEO, Mika Lenna, will tear every city apart until he has his werewolves imprisoned once again. He didn't undertake a huge risk just to lose his would-be assassins.

However, the Lucidite Institute's main mission is to save the world from injustices. Now, it's Adelaide's job to find these mutated men and protect them and society, and fast. Already around the nation, wolflike men are being spotted. Attacks on innocent women are happening. And then, Adelaide realizes what her next step must be: She has to find the alpha wolf first. Only once she's located him can she stop whoever is behind this experiment to create wild beasts out of human beings.

Lone Wolf, #2
Rabid Wolf, #3
Bad Wolf, #4

www.ingramcontent.com/pod-product-compliance
Lightning Source LLC
Chambersburg PA
CBHW050238110726
47898CB00007B/2186